THE WILD DROVER IN DANGER

A
JACK RUTHERFORD
ADVENTURE

Published in paperback in 2024
by The Robinson House Writers

The Robinson House Writers
Arthur Robinson House
13-14 The Green
Billingham TS23 1EU

Cover illustration by Vanessa Wells.

THE WILD DROVER
IN DANGER

A
JACK RUTHERFORD
ADVENTURE

KEN BRAITHWAITE

I am most fortunate to enjoy the targeted enthusiasm of our extended family in my writing which gives me great comfort.

Gillie Hatton is firmly in charge once the manuscript is prepared and her work as mentor, editor and publisher gives me great confidence to go forward.

My Doreen is there always to cajole, encourage, remind and remember when I falter. My loving thanks to a wonderful partner.

To Marcia + Colten

with my best wishes.

Ken

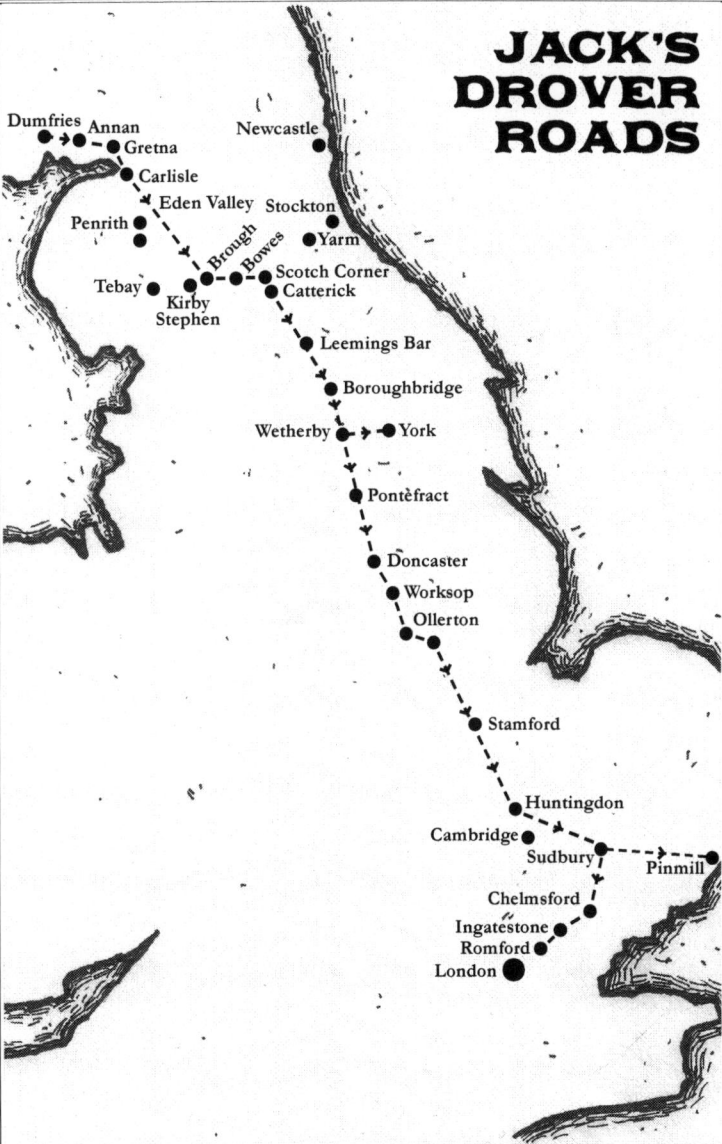

JACK'S
DROVER
ROADS

CONTENTS

CHAPTER 1
CHALLENGE FOR MY PRIZE BULL

To be trapped in the office with books and papers needing all my attention was not my idea of fun. Looking out of my office window to the long drive leading to the house was giving me a tantalising view of my land and the activity going on and I longed to be outdoors again.

My early morning sword practice was a welcome break but then it was head down to concentrate on figures and sums. The fact that I was making money was some compensation but I really longed to be outdoors.

Perhaps I needed to employ a clerk to carry out these accounting duties and I decided to discuss this with Giselle when we met for lunch.

Until then, I sharpened a fresh quill, dipped it in the ink well and continued my task with figures bouncing off the page.

I was briefly distracted from my accounting task by taking a break and reading the local and county news. Newspapers have appeared occasionally in the local town, in the shape of the Cumberland and Westmorland

Gazette and it was in there that I could gain some insight into happenings outside my local view.

The newspaper mentioned the increasing violence associated with cattle theft, to which I could add much interesting detail, but won't. Additionally, it mentioned the feelings of unrest throughout the country following the French Revolution. Giselle and I own tracts of land in France where a former smuggler friend of mine is now in charge of our small estate. I made a note to write for up to date details on our affairs.

Here in England, it was being suggested that there were many movements afoot that disseminated hatred of the nobility and these even included the new Methodist Church whose preachers are looked on with alarm by many in authority. They have actually been heard speaking in this area of Westmorland.

Reading further in my few moments of leisure, I saw that some notorious cattle bandits, the Crozier family, were reported to be active in the area. These are direct descendants of border Reiver families, the worst of that scurrilous bunch and much feared in the cattle business. It was alleged they had an allegiance to France from time immemorial. I almost wanted them to dare try their trade hereabouts… that would be more interesting than books and accounts.

My name is Jack Rutherford. I am the youngest of five children and decided to follow my father into the cattle trade as a drover. At the young age of fifteen, I was sent to learn my trade in Scotland. I'm now twenty-four years of age, 6ft tall, occasionally clean shaven at home and after a very successful and dangerous cattle drove and land speculation in Stockton-on-Tees, I am reasonably well off. I funded my first purchase of cattle by a mixture of hard work and some smuggling of tobacco and tea.

Along the way I met my wife Giselle after she helped me after an accident on the moors involving robbers when we defeated some difficult men and left them to their fate. We have a small son, Giles, who I rescued from kidnappers last year with the help of an enterprising lady in York who is now a bosom friend of my wife's.

Ridley House, which I purchased with the proceeds of my land sale, stands in about two hundred and sixty plus acres of land to the east of Brough under Stainmore, the town where I was brought up, more normally referred to as Brough. This is on the main route for cattle moving from the eastern and central parts of Scotland, making for the lucrative markets in England. Farming is now a mainstay of the estate but our pasture is of great benefit to the constant droves of cattle that need to bed down for a day or two after the long walk from Scotland. They tackle the difficult Stainmore Pass, onward to Scotch Corner and then onto the Great North Road making south. Our reputation of good accommodation for men and beasts gives us a steady income stream.

Jeremiah and Henrietta (Hetty), the previous owners, were invited to stay here when I completed the purchase as they had a good bond with Giselle. They were joined here by my parents. It's a big house and I now employ

3

servants to help in running the estate and to assist with catering when Giselle has her monthly Tea Soirees for the local gentry.

Into this busy house you must also note Giselle's activities in dressmaking and the purchase from the drovers of the knitted goods they make as they travel south. Giselle sells these in markets locally.

My dairy herd continues to grow, with some sheep being successfully reared and sold as well, so inevitably there are books and journals to maintain and my accounts to complete and worry over, all housed in my office that I now find being used far too often.

My reading of the newspapers was interrupted delightfully when Giselle came into my study clutching a large garment, kissed me briefly and suggested I looked more scruffy than ever and needed 'bringing up to date', whatever that meant.

I soon found out. My dress code at home is shoes or boots, stockings, woollen breeches, a long flowing shirt over which I wear a dark black broadcloth three quarter length jacket and of course a cravat. This is the suggested garb apparently for a Squire and that is the status I appear to have acquired.

Giselle's large garment that she had made, was a yellow coloured three quarter length jacket which she suggested I should now wear to 'look smarter'.

Dutifully I shed my coat and tried on this effeminate-looking item which fitted me perfectly, regrettably so.

Amid much smiling and feminine approval, I left the damned thing on, swearing that at the first opportunity I should somehow have it disappear.

Dressed like a dandy, I ventured outside to see what the reaction would be from my colleagues and sure enough my farm manager, Josh Liddell, came over, grinning like a jackass, and putting his hand on his waist, bowed to me and swept his hat off in a courteous manner saying, "My Lord and Master," then fell about in hysterical laughter. I joined in. There was no doubt I looked 'very pretty'.

We discussed matters at length about my herd and the cattle ready for market. I asked how his son was managing with the sheep and was assured all was well. In fact, some of the last year's lambs, particularly the tups, could be considered for market too.

Morning post was infrequent and very novel. Letters arriving in Brough were collected as and when any of my staff were available and today was such a moment. Josh had been in town and post was waiting for me.

This particular letter, written in copperplate hand on the envelope, looked to me as though it had been tampered with. Josh remarked that he had spotted that and reported it to the clerk who had waved his hand in dismissal.

Once back in my office, I opened the letter and found to my delight that it was from the farmer I had met in York cattle mart where we had discussed the need for good breeding bulls to improve milk yield.

Mention had been made of the York dairy farmers

wanting to identify a good breeding bull to go to stud. I'd mentioned Hector, my crazy bull, and his good pedigree (a little optimistically) and his prize winning in Penrith, failing to mention I had provided the prize and that the bull had killed his next owner, which was my intention.

My dairy farmer appeared to have spoken at length to his neighbours and they were anxious to have the bull brought to York and fees for stud were mentioned which made the proposition very attractive to me. Hector is crazy, almost uncontrollable but he is a magnificent example of a Galloway bull and although I should really have had him destroyed after the goring incident, he was so well proportioned that I allowed him to be kept alive.

One major problem is that Hector will only obey one man and that's his handler, Josh Liddell, who talks and hums quietly to the damned great beast and he follows him dutifully and behaves perfectly. But God forbid anybody else who gets in the same barn or field with the bull. He goes berserk. You can imagine the fun and games we would have taking him down to York but it could be done, particularly as part of a drove herd with careful management.

Going back outdoors, I spoke at length to Josh and we agreed that the bull could make the journey and Josh would remain with him at all times whilst about his business in York.

Back indoors, I penned a letter to my York farmer and arranged for it to be taken for posting. I then reluctantly went back to business and was going through my books when I heard a knock on my office door, which when opened, brought a local young scallywag to my attention.

Nervously, the boy handed me a piece of scrap paper marked in pencil for my attention, saying, "I will be beaten, they say, if I don't give this in to your hands," and he ran away, out of the house and down my long drive without a backward glance.

The paper given to me by the urchin stated that the Crozier family intended to take my bull off my hands and I was to deliver him to them at a stated location. It was written that they may consider paying me.

It further stated that when I came to the place mentioned, which was an abandoned property on the very edge of the moors, I would be under the rifle sights of one of the hidden brothers, an expert shot, and any skulduggery on my part would bring an immediate death. I knew this stretch of land that almost bordered my own property and I had often wistfully looked at it and its access to the open moors. I hadn't realised it belonged to these bandits.

I was to depart immediately with one other person and be unarmed.

The Croziers... They had never attempted to cross my path and although I knew of their reputation, through the newspapers and local gossip, we had never met.

Inherent in this was the matter of my family and having once experienced a kidnapping I did not intend this to happen again although that could be implied here.

There were apparently three members of this Crozier

family, a father and two sons, so I could anticipate that one son would be the rifleman and I would be met by the two others. How to outwit them...?

But of more concern... what had prompted them to go head to head against me knowing my reputation for swift action when threatened? Could there be an underlying reason for this provocation? I would have to keep my wits about me.

I penned an immediate letter to the Justice of the Peace in Brough, dating and timing it and setting out clearly just what had happened. I copied the written message and enclosed the original and told the JP that I was complying immediately with the request but asked him not to alert the town authorities as it could put my family in danger.

I made it clear that I would take all necessary precautions but would defend myself if put in mortal danger.

One of my boys was summoned, given the letter and a fast horse with instructions to hand deliver the message into the JP's hand and get a receipt. Another boy on horseback would accompany him for safety.

Josh Liddell joined me then. I gave him both letters to read and he agreed with me that the letter from the farmer in York had been opened, the contents revealed to a Crozier accomplice and we now had a problem.

We collected the bull and set off immediately, I still dressed in my new yellow jacket, and we made good progress with Hector apparently enjoying the jaunt and keeping up with us as we walked briskly the short mile to the suggested meeting place which was among hilly countryside with fields and trees, perfect for a rifleman to be hiding in.

As we neared our destination, I remarked to Josh that this would make excellent grazing for Swaledale Sheep if we could negotiate with these rascals.

Josh had been on many droves with me and had experienced living under the hedges to guard our herd. He was a good man to have in a tight corner, which we were about to enter. I gave him some of my ideas about how we might succeed against these odds and he agreed with my tactics. We were both aware that these Croziers were ruthless killers and our chances of survival would depend entirely on how we acted in concert without others being aware.

Sure enough, we came to the derelict cottage which had a small enclosed garden at the rear with what appeared to be a substantial wall round it, ideal for my purposes.

Nearing, we were told to stop close to the building and Crozier senior and a son appeared, both with long swords. Hector was snorting and rearing, just as I had suggested to Josh previously, and a look of real fear came to the eyes of the villains.

I shouted, "My suggestion is we put this bull in that walled garden for you," and thankfully they agreed. We walked through a shattered door into the wrecked house and out of sight of the rifleman.

With difficulty we manoeuvred the bull through the thankfully wide door and pulled him prancing and kicking into the very enclosed former garden space where we pushed the Crozier son into the yard and barred the door.

Screams and blood curdling yells of terror came from the enclosed yard as Hector attacked.

Crozier senior had smiled briefly in triumph as his son was left with the precious bull and then listened in horror and dropped his guard as Hector gored his son repeatedly.

Dropping the sword, he ran to the door but it was short work for Josh and I to disable the rascal, remove his sword and leave him well battered but still sensible, lying on the floor.

I removed my gaudy jacket and hat, roughly removed Crozier's coat and hat and replaced his garments with mine. Whilst he was still groggy from the beating we had given him, and ignoring the death screams from the garden, we pushed Crozier senior, dressed in my clothes, out of the front door where he staggered forward for a few steps then stared aghast at the clothes he now wore and rose up screaming as the bullet hit his chest. He died immediately.

Sounds from the garden had ceased and at a word or two from Josh, the bull, covered in blood, calmed down.

We encouraged Hector to come out of the garden, back through the house and into the front of the house to await proceedings.

By this time we both had Croziers' swords and hid behind the ramshackle door. A joyful shout of "Hurrah" and "Got you, you bastard" gave us our first inkling of the arrival of the third marksman son and it was as he turned the body of his father over and screamed that I leapt out and struck him a fatal blow to his chest. He fell dead at my feet.

I was weak at the knees with what had happened and I heard Josh retching behind me so I knew he was as affected by these sudden deaths as I was.

It was apparent that the Croziers had not intended us to leave alive but explaining this to the authorities would be difficult.

Both Josh and I were sick again, retching into the bushes when the bull, who was placidly eating grass, swung his head up and roared loudly, bringing us off our knees. Four armed men appeared and gazed in awe at the carnage.

"We have been sent by the Justice to find and protect you from these outlaws, but you seem to have managed. What happened?"

After over an hour of careful investigation, our visitors agreed entirely with our explanation of the slaughter, particularly when we arranged for Hector to revisit the garden scene and his changed demeanour, when left alone near the body, convinced the most sceptical that he was capable of great damage.

My subterfuge with the yellow coat was commented on and we left the bodies where they were. The Justice's party rode off to give confirmation of what they had seen.

Josh and I walked slowly back to Ridley House, shaken beyond belief at the carnage we had witnessed.

Still shaken by the ordeal, we neared our home and I

was very thankful to enter the kitchen, make a big cup of tea for us both and then give Giselle and the gathered staff a very shortened account of the whole affair.

Giselle looked at me quizzically when I mentioned the damage by blood to the lovely coat and although she suggested she could make me a replacement, I have somehow forgotten to remind her about that.

CHAPTER 2
DROVING AGAIN

Some time later, I was again working in my office when I was informed by my staff that a large herd of cattle were coming along the drive. This was unusual as droves normally started about August time and I suspected something was not quite right. Locking my office door, I wandered along to meet the men and the herd.

Father had exiled me at fifteen years of age when the accumulated mischiefs I had arranged became just too much for him. The unfortunate episode with the large male pigs, supposedly in my control, running amok through the packed stalls in Brough Market Place, caused a lot of damage which cost me three nights in the police cells plus a hefty fine from the Magistrates that father very reluctantly paid.

I was immediately packed off to learn my trade as a drover in Scotland. By good chance Dougal MacPherson was in the area so I was placed in his care as one of father's oldest friends, a highly respected drover, based on the shores of Loch Tay in Scotland.

The man approaching was none other than my old

tutor and my heart was bursting with joy to see that hard Highlander again. Because hard as he was, he taught me such a lot and I killed my first cattle thief whilst defending him when we collected his stolen herd from foolish robbers.

Walking quickly towards him, we shook hands and embraced while I welcomed him most heartily to my small estate. Dougal, in Highland kilt, turned and addressed his similarly clad band of ruffians to put the beasts in the stance and find him in the wee house for further instructions.

It occurred to me that a more capable bunch of rogues would be hard to assemble this side of the border and I could only speculate what the reaction would be in our town of Brough.

With my arm around Dougal's shoulder, we walked towards my house whilst I asked about Peggy, his wife, who had spoilt me as though a son whilst I lived with them. She was as well as could be expected, he said, and sent me her fondest love.

As we reached the main door of the house, Giselle came down the steps, ignored me and immediately asked Dougal if I had made him properly welcome.

Assured by him that that was the case, she asked to be introduced to the hardened gnarled Scot and immediately kissed him on the cheek, much to his delight, escorted him in to the reception hall and led him by the hand to the kitchen where she set about making tea and finding biscuits.

Mrs Blenkinsop, our housekeeper, and Dolly Denham the cook were swept aside and told to sit down. It appeared that Giselle was firmly in charge and she had decided, to my delight, that Dougal would be spoilt rotten whilst under our roof.

From that happy beginning, we enjoyed tea, biscuits and a long talk about the journey from Loch Tay to Brough, the health of Peggy, the bunch of scallywags he had brought over the border and the constant danger of thieves and robbers on the road south.

Giselle carefully steered the conversation round to him reminiscing about my long stay in Killin and his teaching me the ways of a drover. Much interesting detail emerged and would have caused me to blush perhaps but at that moment my parents came back and Dougal and George fell about laughing and recalling previous misdeeds which even my mother Mary found interesting and we all laughed a lot.

Dougal's men had been allocated accommodation in our Drovers' Lodge but to his delight and surprise, he was shown by Giselle to the main guest room and it was suggested we all enjoyed dinner that night at 7.30pm.

Our meal over, Dougal and I went outdoors mainly so he could smoke his pipe and we could check that all his crew were warm, well fed and watered.

Walking together, we talked at length. I explained my good fortune in a speculation on land in Stockton-on-Tees that had led to my present property and he was both impressed and delighted.

Then the bad news, he was going no further with his herd.

I was taken aback and couldn't help but say, "Dougal, what's your problem? You have a strong team, a good eye for the ground and you love the road as much as I. What's causing this change of heart?"

"It's not just thieves and robbers anymore, Jack." Dougal looked serious for once. "All the long journey down here, all we've been hearing are rumours of drovers south of here being robbed of everything and being left in a field alive, just, unable to remember what caused their misfortune. Now, I'm done with that kind of danger… but you?"

He knew me too well.

"Now, Jack," he said, clapping me on the back, "I can do you a great favour here. I know you're not short of money but I know that look in your eye, lad, so I am going to be very generous and let you take my herd to York. They're expected in fourteen days."

I thought back to the stack of paperwork in my office. He was indeed doing me a favour. But I wasn't going to make it easy for him.

"Alright, Dougal, how much does it stand you at?" I asked.

So began the long protracted discussion about huge expense, the cost of feed, low margins, all the usual preamble that I was now very familiar with but eventually we settled on a figure and we shook hands. There was a definite twinkle in both our eyes.

Two days later Dougal and his band of men departed with much hugging and fond farewells from Giselle and some of the other ladies I noted. We shook hands and he wished me well and meant it.

After a brief discussion with Giselle, I gathered my usual drovers, Dag, my wolfhound, and Duncan Brooks, my registered drover, he being over thirty years of age, married and with a piece of paper saying who he was. I remained firmly in charge, as always. I had the money and the only horse.

Dag was a killer and would only obey me. I had found him half dead with a dirk through his front leg, pinning him to a tree. I rescued him, taught him to drove cattle very cleverly and we were a close pair.

After so long sitting inside with books and accounts, the open road beckoned...

CHAPTER 3
TO YORK

Leaving is always difficult, farewells to Giselle, Giles, my parents, friends and staff, and then gathering the cattle.

These were the small black kylies, so called as they are often swum across from the Highland islands and the Kyles of Bute and they had grazed hungrily all the way through to England, fattening a little on the way with good roadside herbage. Having settled in my fields for four days, they were reluctant to move.

This is where good dogs play a vital part in any drove and, with much clamour and noise, the herd was assembled to my satisfaction and we commenced our journey.

Gradually we settled the cattle into a regular routine of ten miles travel per day, two days rest for the beasts and we headed for York City. Three hundred cattle can spread over a long stretch of road and it is always difficult to maintain steady progress without tiring the beasts and of course we had to ensure a steady supply of water from remembered sources. Despite the early season for movement, the weather held and our days were pleasant travelling through a very beautiful part of England, the County of Yorkshire.

Near Easingwold on the way to York, I became concerned that the rear cows were falling back constantly and from long experience this would be when a quick raid would separate two beasts that would be driven off quickly through encroaching woodland.

I decided to gallop back, calling my wolfhound Dag to follow me, realising that my fears were well founded as I approached.

In the near distance, three men sprang from a gutter, felled my young man at the back of the herd and separated two fine animals which they whipped away as they ran for the cover of the nearby woods.

We immediately gave chase and I encouraged Dag who beat me to the first thief and ripped open the scoundrel's leg. The thief fell, screaming.

I galloped on, drew my short sword and hacked the next man down, severing his arm.

The final thief, seeing the swift vengeance meted out to his companions, turned in defiance, brandishing a spear with a steel tip and remained standing, offering combat.

At my command, Dag sat and watched and waited. I dismounted and left my horse well out of the way.

My aggressor was a tall dark haired wild looking man, probably a former soldier as he had chosen his defensive position very well. Trees surrounded him on three sides and my only approach could be from in front of him, and his lance was indeed long and lethal. Had I a pistol I would have shot him without mercy. There is no give and take with these deadly thieves.

To close with him would be lethal and I considered my options. I had a short sword but in my boot top I carried the dirk that had pinned Dag to the tree when I found him. It made a very useful throwing knife as well. So be it.

My cautious slow approach was intended to make the man nervous and he stabbed the air around me as I dodged about, testing his resolve. I bent, found a large stone and threw it high in his direction and he looked up. I then took the dirk and threw it very hard, straight to his heart. My aim was true, he stared confounded at the wound and then fell dead.

Dag was all for tearing into the remains but I forbade it, quickly gathered and mounted my horse and rode back to see one thief without an arm and bleeding profusely, the other, with a huge gash on his leg, trying to assist him. Such is the life I have chosen that I left them to their fate. Cattle thieves are killers too and leave few traces so I had no qualms about my actions.

Two hours later with my injured young drover riding behind on my horse, we caught up with my herd and gave some gentle care to the foolish young man. His injuries were a blow to the head and the knowledge he had failed me.

His instructions were always to keep all the animals at the rear as close to the herd as possible. A hard lesson learned.

I hoped that the livestock sale in York would still be held on a Monday because as we neared the city, it was Saturday and I had to find safe grazing for my animals to have them in prime condition.

I had visited York sufficient times to know where to find a good stance and having made my selection, I concluded my arrangements and settled the fee.

My drovers wanted paying as the fleshpots of York beckoned so I obliged and decided to join in their festivities which I thoroughly enjoyed and we all found a reasonable accommodation in a city tavern.

Miss Cornelia Elwick, the milliner of York, had stayed with us last Christmas and had inspired Giselle to consider opening a shop to sell her French influenced dresses and attire.

From an early age Giselle's parents had encouraged her interest in ladies' clothing. She remembers the many sketches she left behind after her parents' murder and has frequently drawn images of fashionable clothing as seen in France and now England. She has always insisted that this would be a suitable occupation for her future which I entirely support.

But Cornelia Elwick was also an investigator of considerable skill, so I left a note through her door to say I was in the city and would like to call on her before leaving.

Sunday was spent preparing the cattle for sale, removing clotted hair and making sure they were well fed and watered for Monday's sale.

Prices were good at the auction and I was able to achieve a reasonable profit. Talk in the mart was all about the robberies prevalent in the south where many a good man had lost his money and his livelihood. Frequent mention was made of a lack of suitable good quality bulls for stud.

Despatching my crew to walk home, some wise men a little richer than when they left Brough, I called into the Select Ladies Hat Shop where I was greeted warmly by Miss Elwick who was able to inform me of all my doings from coming in sight of the Minster. Impressive was the word to describe her many informants.

We spoke at length about Giselle and Giles, my son, the possibility of a dress shop and many other incidents that had occurred since we met.

She knew, of course, of the robberies being made against drovers but would not be drawn, despite careful questioning, on the possible reasons but I left convinced she had more information than she was prepared to disclose, a shrewd lady.

I'd paid Dougal MacPherson £10.0s.0d per head for his three hundred cattle, in other words £3,000 and I was convinced I'd overpaid the man but York Mart came good that day. I managed to get almost £12.4s.0d per animal and I was well aware I was carrying almost £3,600 after I had paid off my drovers and overnight costs.

My sensible option was the stagecoach which I knew would drop me in Brough on its way north and that's just what I did, arriving home in two days and in fact passing my walking drovers on the way back.

All my dogs were home when I returned. Once told to "Go home", they retraced their journey at a steady loping run, always stopping to be fed at the same farms they had used on the way down. We pay for that food as a routine matter.

Dag ran down the long road to greet me ecstatically before I walked up to my house where to my surprise and delight, I saw a diminutive figure on a pony riding with a very straight back. Could it be? With the dog by my side, we watched the slow circuit of the small paddock until horse and rider came in to clear view. It was my son Giles, astride a horse and enjoying himself. As he approached me, I saw the huge grin on his young face.

"I'm going to be a drover, like you, daddy."

To say I was proud is an understatement.

CHAPTER 4
KIRKBY STEPHEN AND THE DRESS SHOP

As I approached the house, a man was climbing out of a carriage, arms laden with packages. Curious, I followed him inside through the main hall and into Giselle's room, where she was waiting with Mrs Blenkinsop, who keeps house for us, and is also a seamstress.

Giselle is a gifted designer of both French and English style ladies' wear and her creations on paper are magnificent. It had been suggested by Cornelia Elwick that there could be a considerable demand for her creations once assembled.

I had long suspected that my pack horse friend Reuben Connor had been inveigled into securing and supplying quantities of quality cloth, needles, sewing materials and this was confirmed when I entered the kitchen to find Giselle and Mrs Blenkinsop enthusing over parcels of colourful, exquisite cloth that shimmered in the light.

"Just the very person," exclaimed Giselle with shining eyes. "Reuben has arranged delivery of some of the most wonderful bolts of material that can only have come from France and it's so exciting, Jack. I can actually start to make the dresses that have only been in my plans so far. Might this be a good time to look at the shop?"

My wonderful wife had previously mentioned that she had her eye on a shop which was in nearby Kirkby Stephen.

I mentioned my visit to her friend Cornelia Elwick and the shop enthusiasm returned with an almost religious fervour. I could understand why. Giselle is part French, having had an English mother who married her father in Saint Omer.

France was where her parents held a small estate for cattle and ran a chemist's shop. Giselle's parents were murdered and she was kidnapped to be sold to a monster of a Magistrate. We met when she escaped from her captors and I was able to assist. After we married, I dealt with the men who so mistreated her.

So shortly after my return, I had the pony and trap harnessed and we trotted off in glorious weather. We arrived in style in Kirkby Stephen where Giselle went straight to the selected shop and hoped to start discussions about the premises with the owners.

By a nod of the head, she indicated I could go about my business. She can drive a very hard bargain and is a good negotiator.

I had a little spot of business of my own to conduct. Two months ago, a new to town butcher had called and agreed to buy four prime cows for slaughter. They were top stock for which I reluctantly agreed a price of £12.0s.0d per animal, provided he agreed to let me have the money immediately.

But immediately was now eight weeks back and I knew from enquiries that the man was doing well but had hinted he had bested me in the deal, so I thought I would just call and remind him I needed paying.

It was just before his lunchtime closing for an hour and his shop was very busy indeed but I waited patiently outside, expecting to catch his eye and that he would come outside and pay me. He ventured outdoors at last.

"No," he shouted in a very loud voice. "I can see you scrounging round outside, Jack Rutherford, but I'll pay you when I'm good and ready and not until."

Perhaps he should have paid attention to the looks on his many customers' faces. They were astounded by his rudeness and were probably aware of my reputation which he did not appear to believe.

By this time, I had walked into the shop to say, "I will see you shortly," then turned away and left but in fact I knew that the key to the door remained in the lock whilst the shop was open, so I quietly took the key, pocketed it and left without another word.

Moving swiftly, I scoured the nearby streets and found the wheelbarrow I was looking for. They are a common sight and are left unattended. I moved the barrow and took a nearby sack cloth that was handy.

Come twelve o'clock, the butcher ushered people out and went to lock the door before his lunch break. He tut tutted a little that the key was missing but closed the door firmly and returned to the shop and disappeared into the depths for his lunch.

Slipping in after he left, I took every single knife, blade, saw, axe and cleaver – all the essential butcher's tools – put them in the wheel barrow and left quietly. I covered them with the sack and popped in the nearby tavern for a beer and a pie.

At one o'clock I was outside the butcher's shop with my wheel barrow, still covered with a sack.

Watching with glee, I saw the man scrambling round, looking for the tools of his trade, whilst a huge crowd of people gathered to both queue for meat and watch proceedings.

After ten minutes of real fun, I approached the shop door and in a very loud voice said, "Butcher Frank, I can let you have all your tools and saws back when you give me the £48 you owe me now and don't forget all these people will watch while you clean everything I have put in that barrow."

The first giggles came from the watchers outside then it spread very slowly through all the queue until there was uproarious laughter such that it drew even more people to the shop.

Steadily the queue disappeared, aware that it would be a long time before all Frank's tools were properly cleaned, and they joined the gathering crowd outside and waited. Sure enough, a very chastened butcher came outside and in a loud voice apologised for his remarks and behaviour and handed me some pound notes which I very carefully counted.

Then in measured tones I stated I would never ever sell him cattle again. I firmly believed that he would be effectively ruined in a short space of time.

Back with Giselle, she had discussed matters with the seller and I thought she would be excited but from the frown on her face, I could see that she was angry.

On entering our pony trap, Giselle turned to me with tears of anger in her eyes.

"Jack, that awful person was terribly rude to me and refused to discuss my offer. She stated that as I am French and they lost two sons at Waterloo, they have no wish to do any business with me."

I offered to intervene immediately but Giselle was adamant, I was not to take any action.

Giselle then explained that the hatred of the French as a nation and as individuals was so fiercely evident that further discussion was futile.

I had to console her and suggested that for some time now I had been pondering the merits locally of this region of England compared to, say, York.

My recent visit there had made me realise the possible vast potential that city had compared to Westmorland but the overheads would be considerably higher and should be carefully weighed up.

As upset as she was, Giselle is very smart and she listened. We enjoyed a good debate on the way home on how we could progress.

Once back at Ridley House, we settled Giles down for the night and went into the main room. Sitting before a warm fire, we continued our discussions.

Whilst we were now successful in Brough and had succeeded in our aim of us both creating income, the long term prospects were doubtful. Giselle's Tea Soirees, whilst very lucrative, would not last forever when the fad for tea drinking faded. Similarly, the dress shop we had considered in Kirkby Stephen could never progress to good profits from the few landed gentry we identified as customers, both now and in the future. I was uncomfortable to think that such animosity towards the French could be directed at my wife.

For my part, droving remains at the heart of my endeavours for the moment but a much longer term prospect would be cattle farming, raising prime beef particularly to feed the demands of the growing numbers of people leaving the farms and working in the large towns. On my recent visit to York, I had mentioned to Giselle how successful Miss Cornelia Elwick's Select Ladies Hat Shop was and both she and I had discussed the prospect of Giselle opening a shop in the city.

Whilst in York and other markets and listening to the conversations, it had become apparent that many local farmers were looking to improve their herds with strong healthy cattle using the services of a pedigree bull.

Our Galloway bull Hector, wild though he is, could certainly go to stud in that York region with a good income from stud fees.

All this information I shared with a very cross and uptight wife who dutifully listened. There was a lot to be considered, I thought. We left it like that and retired early to bed.

CHAPTER 5
VISIT OF THE LORD LIEUTENANT

However, the next day, our circumstances changed. Dust forming in the distance always gets my attention as this could be another large herd wanting an overnight stay. Watching with interest, my heart sank when I saw, approaching, a magnificent coach and four with insignia on the coach doors.

My past misdemeanours were about to catch up with me as the rig was the private carriage of the Lord Lieutenant of Westmorland, the Earl of Lonsdale. As the party drew closer, I saw that his companion was none other than another member of the Lowther family, our local Member of Parliament, Henry Cecil Lowther MP.

All powerful is the term that could be used to describe the Lowther family, whose interests strongly supported the local area. This looked serious.

With them in the coach was a thoroughly nasty looking man who appeared to be some sort of general dogsbody helper, possibly acting above his station.

Slowly the carriage turned to stop at my entrance hall and I watched from the window as the helper scurried out, lowered the carriage steps and handed down the two eminent personalities. As the party descended at my front door, I noticed the man carried a sword.

On the local moors are some bodies deep in a black marsh where I had to fight for my life. Giselle, my wife, is aware of this as she was present and helped me dispose of them.

There are other sites in Scotland where I have had to defend my life. Droving is a fierce trade with thieves and robbers at every hand which is why we are allowed, by law, to carry knives, pistols and cudgels for our defence.

With a heavy heart I carefully cleared my desk and locked away all my papers, hoping against hope that I would be able to work on them again soon. But frankly it looked bad.

Putting on a brave face, I rose from my desk, straightened my coat tails and went to greet my unwelcome guests and it was then I noted my wife Giselle had appeared at the front of the house to see what the noise was about.

We introduced ourselves and learned the swordsman was there for protection. His name was Daniel and he certainly overstepped the mark immediately by talking in French to Giselle, asking if she would like to meet him and enjoy the company of a real man.

Giselle's rapid response left him in no doubt about his place but he nevertheless gave me a most condescending look of triumph. Of course he little realised I speak

French. Our son, Giles, is spoken to in both French and English in our house and as a result I have a reasonable command of the French language. But what on earth was this man doing in this company? He was told to keep silent and attend to his duties.

Preliminaries over, I invited the party into my large office where, to my surprise the MP immediately forbade my staff and my wife to enter the room, advising in a loud voice, "We are not to be disturbed," and took his seat at my large desk with his companion.

I took umbrage at this incursion into my personal domain and rose, even more angry at his effrontery, but I was stilled by the Lord Lieutenant with a finger to his lips. I subsided into my chair and sat quietly until we were all seated and the door to my office firmly closed.

Furious, I waited. Having visited the local gaol infrequently, I looked for evidence of handcuffs but found none.

Henry Lowther MP then announced he was sorry for the presumption he had made and offered his profound apology. He then formally introduced the Lord Lieutenant and also Daniel, the rude person who would feel my wrath very shortly. It appeared he was a skilled swordsman and had been employed briefly for their protection on the open roads.

In quiet tones the MP explained that he was attached to the Office of the Secretary of State for the Home Office in a roving capacity and was privy to secrets both national and international.

The Government were well aware of my possible misdemeanours but could not gather sufficient proof to prosecute me. I stayed very quiet.

Daniel sniggered but was quelled by an irate glance from the Earl.

Further, the MP said that my talents for both making money and surviving against considerable odds had been brought to their attention by one of their most successful agents in espionage, who was based in the area.

Mentally I knew this had to be Miss Cornelia Elwick and on reflection I should not have been surprised.

At this point the Earl interjected, "Mr Rutherford, please forgive this intrusion into your wonderful house. Should anybody enquire as to why we are here, you may suggest I was asking if you were willing to sell the property to me, to avoid any awkward questions, of course. But in reality, we are here on a secret and very important matter which we wish to place before you. My cousin here will explain."

The MP continued. "We have a problem to put before you that is of grave importance to Great Britain and I am here, with my colleague, to ask you to consider a very dangerous mission on behalf of the Government whose interests I represent in this matter. Mr Rutherford, in my capacity as a Home Office Minister, I am made aware of the many threats that are made to the well being of our country and I must tell you that they are real. The French Revolution has encouraged many to believe that we, as a country, would be better served with a constitution based on the French ideal of Liberte, Egaility, Fraternity, which quite frankly is a load of complete poppycock."

It did indeed sound like poppycock. I looked to the Earl for confirmation and received a solemn nod, indicating that I should listen carefully.

"However," the MP said, "my sources advise that this dangerous thinking is being actively sponsored by France here in England, as we speak. Movements such as the Primitive Methodists have uncovered serious schisms in society and we are ever watchful of the effects this can have on the population." He paused for dramatic effect before continuing. "A Monsieur Nicolas Bouchard, a known criminal, minor aristocrat, murderer and spy, has been despatched to England to foment dissent among the working class of, for example, Sheffield, Nottingham and other cities. Guy Delavue is the Minister in charge of the French Police Department in Paris and I have it on very good authority that Msr Bouchard was arrested on a trumped up charge and threatened with the guillotine unless he agreed to take on the role of spy and come to England, to organise marches on London, and he readily agreed."

It sounded absurd. More absurd that they were telling me, a common drover. Another nod from the Earl stayed my impatience.

Henry Cecil Lowther MP continued unabated. "Bouchard arrived in England one year ago and made straight for London where he insinuated himself with many revolutionary groups to feel the strength of opinion. He has now formed The Workers' Patriotic Revolt movement and is using this as a front to hold meetings in taverns where he provides food and beer free of charge to those who will join this movement. You may gather that in these desperate times, free beer and food are serious arguments in his favour."

I couldn't argue with that fact and leaned forward, my curiosity growing.

"My problem," the MP said, appreciating my attention, "has been to find out for certain just where his funds have come from. Certainly not from France or I would have known about it, but by a stroke of good fortune our spies in London happened to be in the Smithfield Market where animals are slaughtered for the active London trade."

At that statement, I sat up.

The Earl smiled to himself as if he had the measure of me.

The MP waited a moment for effect then threw in the facts of this story they knew would get me hooked. "One drover," he said, emphasising the word 'drover', "was observed shouldering a large satchel in which he had placed the proceeds of his successful sales and careful note was taken of his movements. It appears he dismissed all his men and dogs after paying them and then proceeded to hire a coach and horses from nearby to take him to his home in Wales. The coachmen and ostlers there greeted him warmly. He has not been seen since and his fate is unknown. We believe a very considerable amount of money was taken from him, somewhere near

£2,300 which would go, we think, to Msr Bouchard, our French spy. This is how he is able to afford such lavish meals and drink to be served to his many followers. Needless to say, Mr Rutherford, none of this information ever leaves these four walls and you are sworn to secrecy please, as are we all. What would your reaction be if we asked you to work for the government and infiltrate or remove this threat to the country. Before you answer, a positive response would encourage us to overlook some alleged nefarious and deadly activities you may have been involved in."

Speech over, the MP regarded me with raised eyebrows.

I had already worked out where this talk was leading and was determined to get the best outcome from these negotiations.

Standing suddenly and surprising my guests, I bellowed, "You have the damned effrontery to question my position as an honourable member of society, throw false allegations about me into these discussions and expect me to put my life on the line for you?"

I continued in this manner for some time, playing the wronged upright person I purported to be and I thought I was doing quite well.

But Henry Lowther MP was immediately on the attack. "For God's sake, Jack, we have you over a barrel and you know it, but your past misdeeds will be overlooked for the time being if you will consider acting as our agent. I'm not saying these items will ever go away completely but should you decide to work for us, we know your reputation and would wish to have a firm hand on your collar if you wander from the course we will set you."

The bastards had me and they knew it. What may not have occurred to them was that the excitement and element of danger inherent in this venture really appealed to me. I subdued these thoughts, but wondered who Daniel was to sit in on this discussion.

I calmed down somewhat. "Gentlemen, supposing I agree to your wild suggestion… how would we keep in touch during these activities?"

Henry explained that I would be immediately invited to the Office of the Secretary of State for the Home Office, there to meet the Chief Clerk in Charge and instructed in the secret world they inhabited and given access to ways of communication and contact. One likely outcome was that a large march on London was suspected and I had to prevent that at all costs by disabling or removing the important players and deliver, with irrefutable evidence, the perpetrators for trial.

Privately, I decided that would not happen, people would disappear but that was my business.

After some more searching questions, I agreed with great reluctance to proceed, at which point, once again, the MP gave me a hard stare and made it abundantly clear I was on my own in this matter as far as everybody else in my household or among friends and acquaintances were concerned.

Then very interestingly, the Earl drew me to one side and in a whispered conversation stated he was in truth very interested in buying Ridley House and my estate and mentioned an eye watering figure for my consideration.

As the meeting was now concluding, I agreed to their suggestion that I make haste for an appointment in London at the Home Office once an official letter had been received and an address was given. Whilst this was being discussed, I quietly strapped on my sword.

Outdoors, I managed to trip the very rude Daniel as we walked and he fell heavily to the floor but was immediately on his feet, turning swiftly and drawing his own sword. His face changed somewhat when my sword followed his from my scabbard and we met, head on, in a fast and fierce clash of blades. He was good. His movements were lithe and precise and he adopted a very professional stance.

Giselle had joined us again outdoors and watched the fierce swordplay with our guests. She appeared most unconcerned, whereas the Lowther family members watched aghast as the fight moved and became ever more quick and deadly.

Tiring of this man's simple attempt at controlling the fight, I swiftly flicked my blade in a move shown to me by a very experienced swordsman and Daniel stared in horror at his damaged wrist and his sword on the ground some feet from him.

Placing my sword point at his throat, I murmured in perfect French, "Si jamais tu comparais a cette maison ou que tu parles a ma femme, je te tuerai." (If you ever appear at this house or talk to my wife, I will kill you).

"Bravo, Jacque, tres tres bon." (Well done, Jack, very very good). This from the Earl who added, "Daniel, you're dismissed, walk home."

The man slunk off with a very sore wrist and a bent sword.

Giselle was thanked by the visitors on her aplomb during the fight and I welcomed the huge kiss my wife gave me in front of our guests. However, before we waved the party goodbye, I took the Earl to one side and asked how long the man Daniel had been known to him. There was a long quiet pause.

"Do you know, Jack, that's a matter that has been on my mind for the last few moments. You have interpreted these events as I have. He was recommended by a political friend in the Home Office for my security but possibly like you, I now believe him to be a French spy. We dwell in deep murky water here. I will have Daniel followed and report back to you on my findings. Well done."

The party left with due haste and Giselle and I entered our house where, out of sight of the servants, I was given another very long romantic kiss.

CHAPTER 6
OFFICE OF THE SECRETARY
OF STATE FOR THE HOME
OFFICE, LONDON

Shortly after the visit of the MP and Lord Lieutenant, I received in the post a very formal letter inviting me to London and the Home Office.

As I left my home in Brough, I realised I was now working in strict secrecy for the British Government against radical influences which were many and varied throughout the country.

I had been informed by this hand delivered letter that I was to take a named coach to London where I would be met and escorted to an address that was a government department concerned with protection of the realm.

With a strange explanation to Giselle and instructions about the running of my estate, I left for London. Wearing my frock coat and top hat, I made my way by carriage to Brough where I booked and gave my luggage to the safety of the coachman and joined the named London-bound stagecoach. It is always a stuffy cramped journey to the city and it took the usual three days of boring travel to reach my destination.

Stagecoach travel throws you into the company of many strange and varied people and I spent the next few days avoiding prolonged discussion, ate alone where possible, slept comfortably and was relieved to reach London despite the filth and stench all around the roads leading into the city.

Delivered eventually and very wearily to the Coach Station, I hired a Hansom cab as instructed and was relieved to be delivered to my hotel for a good bath, a long meal and a sound night's sleep.

Next morning my destination was to a part of the Home Office but in reality an address in a nearby street unremarkable in its appearance. I had been told to look for a particular brass plaque announcing the premises of an import/export company and having found it, I knocked on the heavy door.

As I entered, two burly but polite men moved me to an alcove and checked me over for weapons, which they removed, then surprisingly one of the men questioned me closely about my background and contacts before I was escorted up a flight of stairs to a rather large office.

Behind the desk of an office door marked Chief Clerk, a large well-dressed man continued to write with his quill pen whist I stood motionless. Minutes passed with no acknowledgement of my presence, so I walked out.

In seconds the man bound from his desk and followed me shouting, "Rutherford, stop."

I kept walking and heard footsteps rapidly nearing. Timing it correctly, I stopped, turned, confronted him full in his florid face and said, "It's Mr Rutherford or sir, and I will not stand for your petty attempt at superiority."

A bad start, I thought, but my contact burst out laughing. "You are exactly as described, Mr Rutherford, for which I am most thankful. Forgive my brusque methods but I needed to test your mettle. My name is Willoughby, by the way."

We returned to his office and once seated, he carefully explained to me the implications of my role, the parameters within which I would work and stressed repeatedly the dangers inherent in this task. We spoke at length and I was frank with him about my background and abilities to which he nodded, as though I merely confirmed what he already knew. He asked if I would care to have a trusted man accompany me on my mission and I suggested I would let him know once I had started the investigations.

Satisfied after four hours of discussion that we were not wasting each other's time, it was suggested I repair to my nearby accommodation, remain indoors overnight and be at this address again next morning at 8.30am. For once, I was so tired that I complied, had a late dinner and retired to my bed. It was just as well because the next day I was informed I had been under surveillance all night.

As arranged, we met again and I was informed how to make contact with the office, how to make contact with the military and also words to use in conversation to hint at my progress. The thoroughness of my briefing and the extent of my involvement could only impress upon me the seriousness of the government's alarm at the possible rebellion that was brewing.

Communications were to be kept to a minimum but must be maintained. The suggestion put forward was that I would write to an address – 22 Tufton Street, London – marking the letter 'For the attention of the Porter'. I would sign as 'RX' and any response would only be valid signed 'XR' which seemed stupid to me, but so be it.

One final item remained. I was told, and this must never be put in to writing but to be committed to memory, that throughout the country the police forces had been given a code word that was to be used most sparingly to make contact direct with the Chief Constable of the County in the event of an emergency. This was two letters and two numbers, in my case Z8Q9.

I was to present these numbers written on my hand at any police desk and await a reaction after rubbing my hand clean.

No words were to be spoken except to the Chief Constable in whose presence alone I could explain my concerns which would be communicated very quickly to the Home Office desk appropriate to my mission. Serious business.

I was then given a brief of what I had to do, when. It would be dangerous, I had no doubt of that, but the importance to national security and the crown was beyond doubt. I could not refuse.

My briefing complete, I was escorted in a carriage

to my rendezvous on the Royal Mail coach, taking me quickly north to home and danger.

It was eleven days after I left that I returned home from my city experience a much wiser and learned person. My role had been explained, my dangerous mission clarified and methods of keeping in contact and reporting defined. A surprising number of people were available but what came as a considerable shock was the proposed use of the army to come to my aid if the march on London seemed likely.

CHAPTER 7
YORK

Giselle was very curious about my visit to London and questioned me closely over the next few days but I kept my wits about me and explained that the Lord Lieutenant wished to see me in London about purchasing Ridley House. That set the tone for many long conversations that evening and I mentioned York, its environs and wonderful shopping opportunities, and the frowns appeared again along with the frosty atmosphere. She was obviously worried about the reception she had received in Kirkby Stephen.

But I made it clear I wished us to visit York as a family, taking Giles with us, and have a look at what was clearly a very important and busy city.

With considerable thought and discussion, we made the decision to visit York, meet Cornelia and discuss the prospect of moving south to that large city.

It took two days to travel by coach as we needed to stop overnight for young Giles to enjoy a reasonable night's rest.

Immediately on arrival after our overnight stay in a hotel, Giselle insisted we visit Cornelia Elwick at her Select Ladies Hat Shop near to York Minster. We took a carriage and, with Giles along, we bowled to a stop and Giselle flew into the shop in a whirl of long skirts and petticoats to meet Cornelia. Giles was in my arms as I paid for the carriage and headed for the shrieks and laughter that indicated Giselle had found her good friend.

Once indoors, I put down Giles who ran to the girls and was swept up, kissed and made much of, to his delight. Then Cornelia came over and allowed to me to give her a kiss and suggested we all needed to talk.

Needless to say, with her army of contacts, she knew of our arrival, where we had stayed and the possible reason for our visit. Cornelia is the spy, I do believe. If she worked for the British Government, she could have mentioned my name to the powers that be regarding the possible Insurrection Movement that was preying on the drovers. She was both extremely attractive and formidable, possibly why her and Giselle got along so well.

Over tea and biscuits in the darker recesses of the fashionable shop, I explained that we had now received an offer for Ridley House and the surrounding estate that we found most attractive.

Further, I mentioned I had thought long and hard about relocating to the York area to eventually become a dairy farmer. Giselle mentioned she had almost signed up to open her Ladies High Couture shop in Kirkby Stephen but that I had prevailed on her to consider York as a more realistic location for her expensive gowns and dresses. She also mentioned that another option was being considered but made no further mention of it, unusually.

Cornelia expressed her delight at the prospect of her friend possibly coming to live and work in the area and immediately they started making plans to visit sites in the town.

This could work out rather well, I thought, so as the ladies ordered a carriage to look at prospective shop locations, I gathered young Giles and walked to see my good friend and Solicitor, Aubrey Percival in his office near York Minster.

Giles stared in wonder at the urchins in the street, the braying dogs, horses and carts moving goods, the stench of unwashed bodies and filthy gutters and the general bustling of a huge city in full flow. Tightly holding my hand, he remarked, "Daddy, it's very smelly and horrid. Do we have to stay or can we go back to Mummy?"

I explained, "Giles, this is a very big city where people come to work and you will see some of this work shortly, I hope, so keep your eyes open."

On arrival at Aubrey's office, unannounced, I was delighted when his staff informed me he would shorten his meeting that was in progress and would I take a drink and await him in his anteroom where Giles was once again the centre of attraction to the young ladies who served tea and biscuits to the young man and I.

Aubrey joined us within twenty minutes and we brought each other up to date. We had both made a considerable amount of money on an investment in land next to the River Tees in Stockton and this had brought benefits and a firm friendship.

As we talked, Giles began to get noisier and noisier. Aubrey smiled and called to two of his young office girls to take the boy into the garden for games, enabling us to concentrate.

I mentioned to Aubrey my thoughts about dairy farming in the area and he immediately agreed this would be a sound investment. During my previous visit to the city, I had made a good sale in the market and was approached about my prize bull Hector who, it was suggested, might be available to stud. At stud he would command a good fee and I discussed this and the prospect of a suitable farm to purchase.

Aubrey asked me to wait a moment whilst he ferreted round in his office and produced a file which he placed on the table before us. Aubrey's client was at retiring age and was interested in selling his large farm, Campleshon Grange, which comprised seventy-four acres of prime land near a village which was but a ten minute carriage ride from Bishopgate Street, a very popular shopping area.

After changing some appointments, Aubrey and I picked up a reluctant Giles, ordered a carriage and drove to the village after collecting Giselle at the hat shop.

Ignoring the large house on arrival, I instructed the driver to tour round the land, first along The Avenue and then, returning to the main road, we traversed along

Campleshon Lane. These were well fenced fields, filled with healthy cows and the prospects looked good. We retraced our steps to the main road again and viewed the field to the east of the main road which led down to the River Ouse. It all looked to be in excellent order and possibly capable of expansion.

Giselle insisted we looked at the large Campleshon Grange next and we stopped outside while Aubrey called and explained our presence. We were invited in and made most welcome. Yes, they would like to sell but it would not be cheap. We were in Yorkshire, of course.

Nothing was decided but my impressions were favourable that we could negotiate with confidence. I had noted both the dimensions of the Grange and the nearby building which would house some further family if I could tear Josh and Margaret away from Westmorland.

Back along Bishopthorpe Road, I watched Giselle take a growing interest as we neared the city and some lovely shops appeared. Her interest grew and she requested the carriage driver to slow down as she neared what turned out to be Bishopgate Street.

"Stop," she demanded and quickly left the carriage and walked to a very smart small shop and entered before we could react.

Aubrey and Giles looked at me for guidance but I shrugged and said, "She is French, you know, and occasionally erratic," which they accepted.

We waited for a few minutes before my wife returned and suggested to Aubrey he may wish to join her and ask to meet the vendors and arrange the details. She had her new shop!

God bless him, Aubrey took it in his stride, collected his top hat and together they practically skipped to the shop.

Giles and I sat together in the carriage, awaiting the return of Giselle and Aubrey when my son made an interesting remark. In a small voice, he whispered, "Can we go home now?"

That small remark made me think very seriously about the next few years and our prospects.

Did I really want to leave Brough? We were very settled there, with family about us, good friends nearby and a long family commitment to the area through my parents. We were making good profits from droving and the farm and despite the Lord Lieutenant's snide comments about my past, I could hold my head high as a Squire of the area.

Were we making the right decision in coming to York or was there a compromise to be made?

Giselle and Aubrey returned but not in the happy manner I had imagined. Giselle plumped herself on to the carriage seat and gave me a considered look. Aubrey, when he settled in the carriage and told the driver to move on, gave me a cursory shrug of the shoulders. I wasn't sure what was going on.

Within ten minutes we returned to Aubrey's office near York Minster and after long farewells and promise of correspondence, we bade good bye.

Using the same carriage, we set off and Giselle explained to me what had happened.

"My accent was immediately commented on," she said, brushing down her skirts as she sat, "and matters became very frosty from then on. There is the distinct anti-French feeling again and suddenly the price of the place rockets to a point where I realised it was silly to continue to speak, so I turned and walked out of the place."

I didn't blame her. In fact, I was quite proud.

So, tired, somewhat deflated and anxious to get a small young boy safely fed, washed and to bed, we returned to our hotel. Giselle and I, after a light dinner, were about ready to retire early for a prompt journey north to home when I felt the need to do some serious thinking about the future.

Our hotel was near the centre of town and the market had occurred that day so there would be farming folk still in the inns and taverns. Despite Giselle's suggestion of 'an early night', I left her with a good book, collected my coat and walked to the nearest noisy inn, entering the bar and ordering a pint of beer.

Yorkshire farming folk abounded and I was quickly assimilated into their company where every issue connected with the land was mentioned and considered.

As the night drew on, I broached the subject of my Galloway bull for use at stud and there was a lot of serious interest, sufficient that I noted down the names of those who would like me to write with more detail. The reasoning being that a good dairy herd producing milk would see increasing sales in the city area and its surroundings.

Walking back to the hotel that late evening, strolling beneath the trees in the flickering candlelight from town houses I realised how encroaching the town was compared to our home but I also foresaw the potential of a dairy herd in the vicinity of the town or access to it.

Deep in thought, I strolled past our hotel and continued with some deep contemplation. There was talk of a great revolution coming with the new steam engines that were mentioned in the newspapers, and with the enclosures, many families were leaving the land and coming to the cities and towns for shelter and work, but what effect would this have on my lifestyle and farming interests?

We had the land and property in France and all the letters I received from Serge told me he was expanding our cattle herd with good profit.

But what of these steam engines? My farming companions in the tavern that evening were dismissive of my comment that an 'engine' might better move cattle and scoffed at the notion but could they be wrong? It was now 1825 and the newspapers mentioned a Darlington Railway running along steel rails. I wondered if that was to be the future.

Hard as the droving life had been, it had given me a good start in life and I had made some reasonable investments in my land purchases in Westmorland. But what of the next few years?

Farming seemed to hold good promise, both in the

purchase of land and the building up of a herd but should this be cattle only or was my land capable of raising sheep?

Talk this evening was of a Swaledale breed being introduced into that part of Yorkshire with sound ewes caring for their offspring and coming to market at a good price. These sheep were very hardy and remained outdoors in all weathers even through winter and could form the basis of a good broad farm and of course my skills in moving animals would take my stock to market.

I resolved to discuss this with Giselle but on my return, she was fast asleep in bed where I gently joined her after my toilet.

Next morning, after an early breakfast, we took a carriage to the coach yard and boarded to begin the long journey back to Brough and over the next two days we discussed at length just what we wanted from York and compared it to home. Some very interesting points emerged.

Giselle's ambition was to establish a very high class dress making establishment, catering to the 'Quality' who could afford the huge prices she intended to charge. As she observed, York held far more 'Quality' than Westmorland in its entirety and that was her market, but the experience with the French-hating shopkeepers had dented her enthusiasm. From my point of view, York held many attractions, good dairy farming prospects, possible droving work and some stud fees for the use of Hector the mad bull.

We discussed at length my thoughts of the previous

evening and Giselle mentioned the purchase of a small herd of Swaledales. We both laughed at our independent parallel thinking and agreed there was an interesting prospect in establishing a cattle and sheep farm.

Rolling along in the stage coach, holding hands and entertaining a fractious Giles, it occurred to me that the stage route we were on ran from York through various stages that always included Brough and what if Giselle opened her shop in Brough, made the dresses to order and shipped them to York for Cornelia Elwick to sell them from her present ladies hat shop. My thoughts were that the designs and plans could be sent in the post, delivered to the shop in Brough and the completed garment placed in a properly made box and delivered within a month.

Pleased with this thought process, I further speculated that a small farm on the northern outskirts of York would attract droving trade for me but also make a base to house the mad bull who could then go to stud. Here the problem would be to convince Josh to move out to a new location.

Then I remembered, his son James was determined to become a stone mason and York had one of the most famous Masons' yards in the country.

These thoughts filled my mind to such an extent that Giselle nudged me in the ribs and asked what I was contemplating. Nothing ventured, nothing gained... I hinted gently at my earlier thoughts, about dressmaking in Brough, Royal Mail delivery of parcels, dresses being shipped out and other muttered ideas then I sat back expecting a furious reaction and a strong French tantrum. Nothing of the sort. Giselle leapt across the carriage and swooped into my arms, kissing and hugging and laughing.

Then very gently and quietly, Giselle asked me to explain and develop my thoughts, which I did and after a long silence it turned out she was having similar doubts about the York venture but had already checked out the possibilities of working in Brough.

By the time we reached home, we had developed the ideas of both a mixed herd of cows and sheep and the investigation of the stagecoach to communicate with Cornelia in York, and we agreed to take our ideas further.

It was then that Giselle informed me that she had a planned Tea Soiree for tomorrow, and that she had a jacket that would be perfect for me.

Of course, I said I was delighted to be at home for such an event. I almost bolted that very night but how could I, when Giselle was so keen for me to wear her new coat...?

CHAPTER 8
TEA SOIREE

Our discussion about both dress making and farming had left me in a quandary. It was Gisselle's wish that I gradually move away from the dangers of droving and become a farmer, selling beef and lamb for market in the big towns. This made good long term sense but I revelled in the dangers of the drove roads and would be most reluctant to give it up. My background as a smuggler was well known locally and my good fortune did not always sit well with certain people.

Mulling over these matters the next day, I strolled around the perimeter of our land and checked on fences, walls and gates for signs of intruders whilst deep in thought.

As I approached our house, Giselle came out to meet me and reminded me that she had one of her Tea Soirees arranged for that evening.

These events started when I successfully smuggled quantities of tea to provide what was then, two years ago, a very important social occasion for local society.

Indeed at these occasions, which had grown over time, a large number of horses and carriages appeared, all needing spaces to move to after depositing their well-dressed occupants. I had large areas cleared for this and made ready for these occasions. The attending grooms were able to remain under cover. In fact it was the drovers' quarters they occupied.

Preparations made with my reliable staff, I made indoors and reassured Giselle that all had been arranged. I was reminded that my dress sense would be tested to the extreme on this occasion as some local gentry had indicated they would attend and I would need to wear suitable attire, new coat included.

That evening saw a stream of horse drawn carriages moving steadily through the entrance gates and making their way to the front of Ridley House to be greeted by Giselle and I with Jeremiah and Hetty as hosts. The latter were the former owners of Ridley House and it was their connection with local society that encouraged many people to attend.

As we waited on our entrance porch to greet our guests, Giselle excitedly informed me that the carriage coming down the drive belonged to no less than Sir John and Lady Penelope Bell who had travelled over from Appleby for the occasion.

This appeared to be a coup for her Soiree among local society and I was warned to look impressed. I tried my very best.

On entering, there was great hand wringing and

flouncing about and I noticed a dark haired man, very well dressed, who took a long time greeting my wife, the conversation all in French.

Moving gently to my wife's side, I enquired of the health of the gentleman, in French, and received a reply in excellent English, asking, "And who are you?"

I curbed my response to a reasonable, "Your host, sir."

After that, I looked hard at the man and waited for his response which came very smoothly.

"Mr Jack Rutherford, how delighted I am to meet you and thank you for your kind invitation today. I have arrived in the company of Sir John and Lady Penelope Bell and they tell me of your exploits both home and abroad which we in France find most amusing."

There are moments when you realise that you are being both examined and tested by a potential adversary and extreme caution suggests an exploration of the enemy's objectives.

"How wonderful to have you visit us after the horrors of Waterloo," I said. "I trust you were not affected by that war or the Revolution that France has experienced."

"My role in the warfare was minimal as an observer but the Glorious Revolution has encouraged me to explore England and get a sense of the feelings here in your green and pleasant land of Ros Bifs."

This was a very dangerous man indeed. An observer of the war could possibly mean a spy and the tour of England a subtle exploration.

As more guests arrived, I bade the man farewell,

realising that I had not even heard his name mentioned, but I was sure Giselle would have his details before too long.

Carriages came, guests arrived and departed and the event passed in a whirr of tea, cakes and social chit chat until carriage lamps were lit, horses harnessed and the whole rigmarole of departing commenced and went on for the next hour.

In that time, I had quietly followed the Frenchman as he toured my property, spoke to my staff and made notes in a small book he carried.

Once we were alone together and enjoying the inevitable cup of tea, I asked Giselle for her opinion of the French guest and was not surprised when she said, "You mean Henri de la Compte? I thought him very creepy and I wouldn't be surprised if he worked for the French Government. He knew all about our land holdings in St Omer and that area. And Jack, he questioned me very closely about your activities too, including your droving movements."

It was disturbing but I needed get back onto my next task, which was to buy a herd of cattle in Scotland, take them to Smithfield Market in London and see what might develop from that dangerous visit.

I changed the subject back to the dress shop. Giselle said that whilst I was away, she would handle the discussions with everybody involved and write to Cornelia Elwick in York, explaining the thinking and asking for her further involvement and clarification of everything in writing.

I left next day with my dogs and men for the long walk to Falkirk.

CHAPTER 9
DANGEROUS DROVE TO LONDON

Falkirk Tryst was my destination where hundreds of Scottish cattle are available for sale straight from the hills and mountains. These cattle are very hardy, half starved and always fatten up very quickly on the long journeys where they enjoy lush pasture on the roadside such as is never seen in their usual environment. But they take a lot of firm handling.

My journey on horseback to Falkirk with some of my drovers went mostly without incident. Our usual taverns were only partly filled with passing drovers and their herds of cattle. We had few fights and little damage to pay for. Mine are a very hardy rough crowd, difficult to control and I freely use my fists to make my point of view very clear but they strangely remain very loyal and take no nonsense from anybody else.

Letters to Giselle had to be carefully given to passing pannier men to be sent by Royal Mail coach as and when I had the opportunity and they cost me some serious money at times. Knowing Giselle had contact from me occasionally gave me great peace of mind.

Nearing the fields holding the black cattle, I became concerned at the number of apparent buyers for the herds and some caution was needed to avoid paying top price.

Habitually, the selling drovers and farmers gather their herds on the outskirts of town in designated fields, then select fifty of the best animals which they take to the Tryst to obtain a price per animal.

I'm wise to this and always find and study these distant animals before I consider bidding for the displayed beasts at the Tryst.

Some of the drovers were known to me and their shady dealings I knew too well.

Wandering on horseback, I was able to assess the cattle properly and two herds of what would be three hundred head in total took my eye. They both stated they came from the area around the shores of Loch Tay which I knew very well but of the two people I spoke to, one had no knowledge of my friend Dougal MacPherson whilst the other much younger man knew him well and described him.

Cattle from the shores of Loch Tay always sell at a good price as they mature wonderfully on the journey south and attract a higher price.

Studying both herds, it became apparent that the younger man's beast were the real thing and I entered into negotiations immediately. Instantly the older drover and two of his men approached and demanded I cease talking to the youngster, who knew nothing and I was to conduct business with them.

Dag, my huge wolfhound, growled ominously but these men took no notice and started pulling on my boots in an attempt to unhorse me.

I was off that horse and into them with my fists in a second, feeling extremely angry. The main protagonist, the drover, was a big man and swung a haymaker at me which I ducked, only to be held from behind by his colleague ready to be punched and beaten into submission. Dag then intervened, bit my assailant's leg to the bone and his scream of pain was deafening.

He let go. Then Dag did exactly the same to the third assailant, leaving me to beat the daylights out of the drover.

His blows were for small street fighting, mine were for the kill and I hit him under his throat at an opportune moment after having some heavy blows from him to my chest and face. He dropped to the ground gagging and that's when I broke his rib with a kick.

Both his companions were by now on the ground in fear of my killer dog and I gave them both a similar treatment.

Staring in awe at the writhing figures on the ground, the young drover was briefly lost for words.

Once recovered, he said, "Dougal mentioned you could look after yourself. Can we get back to discussing a price for these cattle please?"

We settled on £8.10s.0d each which was a fair price to pay and we parted, I having paid him in full and received a receipt.

I rode into the Tryst area, collected my droving team from a beer tent and we quickly took the herd under control and started the long journey that would end in Smithfield Market London in about eight weeks time.

We could travel about fifty miles in a week with reasonable weather and good overnight stances and I had decided to travel down the east coast of Scotland to Berwick and then on across the River Tweed, the River Coquet, the River Tyne and so on to cross the River Wear and then the River Tees.

Danger lurks at the rear of a large drove such as this because straggling cattle that fall behind the herd are a prime target for the occasional local thieves who can make off very quickly with a beast. I kept a constant watch for stragglers, as did my drovers and we were adept at keeping our herd as compact as possible at all times.

During this long move from Scotland and into the Border country, I experienced far more of these attacks than normal. Trade in cattle had remained extremely good despite the end of the war with France but I was aware of the continued malign influence of that country in England's affairs and the incident with the Lord Lieutenant's staff gave me cause for concern. I resolved to investigate this at a moment of my choosing.

The River Tees was a recommended new route to me but apparently took to the high ground where my constant followers of thieves could more easily be seen. We had lost one beast near Berwick and failed to catch the culprits but the robbers who took three beast near Sunderland would not work for many months after we caught them. I failed to question these thieves closely and now regretted that oversight. Were they being paid to harass me?

We made steady progress after leaving Durham City and the River Wear crossing and passed Sedgefield, making the long steady journey to Yarm-on-Tees which I knew of old.

Crossing Yarm Bridge, we moved steadily through the very wide main street, making south for Crathorne and then followed a good drove road, climbing gradually to a gap in the Cleveland Hills called Scarth Nick which rises quickly, as we found on arrival, then we took the excellent Hambleton Drove Road across those wild moors. The tales were correct, this was high ground and visibility was excellent, such that our followers were very exposed and soon disappeared.

An excellent overnight stance was found at the Chequers Inn and next day we set off on a fine autumn morning, making for the next stance eight stiff miles uphill to Limekiln House.

A torrential storm broke as we crossed these moorlands and even the hardy cattle were glad to eventually rest and enjoy good grazing in the rough but adequate stance opposite the overnight accommodation.

Limekiln House was a basic, single storey building with

a deep cellar and good beer. Having paid the halfpenny charge for my cattle and rough sleeping for all my men, I settled down to a pint or two of beer after checking the routine I had agreed for watch keeping on my herd.

At about 10pm I moved out of the bar, checked my sword and dirk were in place and secure, and nodded to my wolfhound Dag to join me. Outdoors, the rain had eased, leaving a cloud riven sky with the occasional glimpse of the moon, a hunter's moon.

All day I had scanned behind us for movement over those vast moorlands and despite the lack of cover, I had become convinced that in the far distance three figures crept furtively forward, keeping pace with my herd.

Panniermen with their donkeys laden with goods for local markets regularly overtake my slowly moving cattle and the mere fact these men had not moved forward made me wary. Had there been any traders coming my way I would have questioned them about these men but that was not to be, so Dag and I would enquire of their intentions in our own way.

Stalking is inherent in my blood, refined by my three years in the Highlands of Scotland and all my skill came to be used that night. The moor was bleak at this height above sea level with few hiding places except undulations in the ground. That night, the wind was from the south west and I had viewed the passing ground with the thought in my mind that should I wish to remain hidden but outdoors then any deep rut out of the wind would give basic cover.

If, as I imagined, the intention was to kill some of my cattle and allow the remainder to flee, the ensuing commotion would allow these men to kill me or some of my men as we searched for our lost beast.

With my hands and face blackened with earth, I left Limekiln House and strode east for half a mile before moving left and creeping slowly for two miles, retracing our earlier route to come to the most likely place for the thieves to lay in wait.

Nearing the location, we bellied down on the ground… yes, both me and the dog, then we crept forward to the place I hoped held our prey. Slowly, ever so slowly, we approached the dip in the ground, expecting at any moment to be challenged or shot. We hardly dared breathe as we closed in and I was fearful it had all been a waste of time as little could be seen so we waited.

Snoring gave them away. They had no lookout posted, they just huddled in their clothing, rifles and swords laid nearby. Each was given a hard blow to the head to render them unconscious then I tied their hands and feet with their bootlaces, removed the guns and swords plus dirks and money then slowly, as they woke, gagged them and then with my knife stripped their clothing and boots off.

It is very cold on those moors, even in late summer, and they soon started shaking, first with fear that I was going to kill them, which was likely and then, as they cooled off, they shook with the intense cold.

Questioned with the gag removed, the apparent leader eventually, after some skilled work with my knife, was able to confirm a French man had paid him handsomely to disable me and scatter my herd.

I left them to their devices and hoped they could attract some attention the next day, if they survived the cold that was.

Dag seemed disappointed that blood was not drawn but we returned to our beds and in my case slept soundly, some £100 richer with the French reward money.

Waking and moving on the next day, I pondered carefully the implications of the knowledge I now had. As we moved the herd off the Hambleton Drove Road and made our way towards York, I gave the matter some thought. Why would a French agent try to prevent me reaching Smithfield Market to sell my cattle when the objective was to rob me of my profits?

Remembering my first contact with the Earl and MP my thoughts dwelt on the man Daniel and his involvement in this matter. Somewhere along the process, my details had been made known to the opposition who were now trying to remove me from the mission. I have a reputation for prompt action and a determination to succeed. Was this sufficient to have me killed?

The only time I had been questioned closely was when I first entered the secret Home Office premises, when one individual had taken an unhealthy interest in my background.

It was likely then that there was a spy in that office and the whole escapade was compromised, unless I could intervene. But how?

CHAPTER 10
COURTING DANGER

Our long journey continued. My topman Duncan Brooke continued to impress me with his skill as a drover, and his ability to foresee difficulties and have men in place ready for any event impressed me greatly. It was when he was in drink that I had problems with him and all the time he was in my employment, I made it clear with my fists that he would not touch any drink.

After the long drop down from the moor road, the herd made steady progress to Easingwold. The route took us to Wetherby and would then continue to Doncaster, Stamford and on the Great North Road heading south. It was at Wetherby that I gave Duncan instructions on the form I wished the herd to adhere to and precisely which overnight stances he should use as I was leaving for a short while.

I negotiated the purchase of a horse and saddle and left for the journey to York that I had decided to take. I needed to alert the Home Office of my suspicions and could hardly write as the letter could easily be intercepted in that small office. But an alternative was to trust to my gut instincts and call to see Miss Cornelia Elwick who, if my suspicions were correct, was in the pay of the government as a spy in the North of England. It would be a difficult discussion as secrecy was at the forefront of these matters and the subject extremely hard to raise without rousing suspicions.

It was some sixteen miles to travel which, with good weather for once, I was able to accomplish in one day, and having found accommodation for my horse and myself, I took an early dinner and asked for an early call next morning.

Once I had breakfasted, I made my way in some trepidation to the milliner's shop in York near the Minster and was knocking at the door for entrance at 9am.

Cornelia's assistant was pleased to admit me and I was escorted to the rear of the shop where hats of all sizes and descriptions were displayed in a dazzling array of colours.

Cornelia, wearing a most becoming dress with a startling décolletage, came quickly over, stood on her tiptoes and gave me a most lascivious long lingering kiss!

My startled reaction brought a mischievous smile to her face as she beckoned me into a nearby changing room, closed the door and again almost threw herself into my arms.

My reaction had been to embrace her and put my arms round her and then I thought of Giselle and I put my arms out in a scarecrow stance and became immobile.

Cornelia dropped her arms from round my neck, took a step backwards and in a most stern voice remarked that I had just passed the test.

I was furious. I stood back and wagged my finger in her face. "Don't ever try that kind of nonsense with me again. My love for Giselle is complete and I am shocked at your behaviour particularly as you appear to be very friendly with my wife."

Cornelia said, "I am very friendly with your wife. She is my closest friend but I wished to test your mettle and I am satisfied you are faithful to her. But at the same time, I am aware you may be going into danger and I needed to see how alert you are to side issues and distractions that may occur."

In one sentence she had confirmed in a roundabout way that she was aware of my mission. Now I had to tread very carefully.

"Just suppose," I said, "that I was entrusted with information of a delicate nature that had to be passed to our government. Could you suggest a discreet way of making that detail known in the correct places?"

She considered my comment for a long time and then remarked in a business-like way, "Proceed, Jack. I know all about your task. What do you need?"

Over the next few moments, I shared with her my misgivings about the infiltration of the Home Office section I was dealing with and together we discussed the likely outcomes. Cornelia would write immediately to her London contacts and the missive would be sent by Royal

Mail coach that day. Only the chief officer would be made aware of these facts, nobody else.

She would inform her contact of my suspicions and suggested that I would wish to take advantage of the previous offer and have somebody alongside me in this venture to continue the task should I be killed. In this way, we decided that secrecy could be maintained.

Cornelia then asked me to accompany her from the ladies changing room back into the main shop where a stunning dress was displayed behind a curtain. Pulling aside the curtain, she indicated that this dress had been received yesterday from Giselle in Brough using the coach service. Once carefully unpacked, the quality of the garment had become apparent and word had quickly spread through the ladies' grapevine.

Cornelia astounded me by saying she had asked and had been paid £50 for the dress for which Giselle would earn £25. That was a man's wage for five years and I was astounded that this could happen, but Cornelia mentioned that the next four dresses to that standard had already been spoken for.

Cornelia agreed to put a note in from me when she replied and I quickly scribbled a few words of delight and encouragement then with a heavy heart to be reminded of home, I set out to catch up with my herd.

Two days riding and I had caught up again, sold the horse and saddle for exactly as much as I paid for them in Wetherby and joined my men.

Along the Great North Road, we carefully managed our herd of three hundred cattle, always stopping for water where appropriate and the beasts grazed constantly on the verges which in early August gave excellent herbage and nutrition. Good management of my herd was a priority because care taken now would yield a better profit at market.

Villages and towns came and went until looming ahead was the steady rise of land over which we must climb to reach our night's destination, Grantham.

It was when we neared Grantham that my problems recommenced.

Our overnight stay was in a stance of some merit with a nearby inn, The Blue Pig, as accommodation for me and those of my crew who were not on watch. Drink was available as well as excellent food. My constant fear was that we were being watched and followed. I could not discount the involvement of the French in my activities and I was extra vigilant.

Sitting quietly in a corner and almost out of sight in the dark, I watched as a very loud mouthed individual pressed drink after drink on my topman who refused at first but eventually succumbed.

Duncan was completely plastered by the end of the evening and the provider of drink had a self satisfied smirk on his face, imagining the chaos that would ensue if the topman was either missing or incapacitated next morning. My fears were well founded. I admit I was scared of the perilous road I was taking but it was my decision and I had to act alone and not involve my crew unnecessarily.

Once the inn closed, I rose from my seat and followed the provider of drink out of the inn and into the surrounding darkness. My eyes quickly became adjusted to the night in time for me to see the man being clapped on the back by none other than the Daniel character I had met at home and fought to a standstill. My suspicions were well founded. Here was proof that I was being followed by somebody in the pay of the French Government intent on my distress.

Nothing could be gained by removing the drink provider but disposing of Daniel would be a delight.

Advising my crew to make Duncan horribly sick and to anticipate my being missing on the morrow, I suggested we stay at the stance all next day to rest the cattle and we would start our journey again at dawn on the day after next.

With that I left their company and found Daniel still in deep conversation with the provider, with much waving of hands and laughter.

Daniel walked away, apparently contented and moved briskly into town where I followed at a distance and found his accommodation. I booked into the same inn and asked for an early call and a good breakfast, for which I paid in advance. I slipped back to our stance, collected my sword and pistol, returned to the inn and slept soundly.

At dawn, I was woken, bathed, dressed and took a table for my morning meal, having strapped on my sword.

Daniel appeared, took his chair at a table and demanded instant attention from the serving maid who cowered at his loud voice and broken English. He hadn't seen me.

I waited. Sure enough, the meal was not to his liking and he threw the food on the ground. It scattered everywhere. None came anywhere near me but the excuse was perfect.

Brushing imaginary food from my jacket, I quietly suggested he should apologise to me. He took the bait, rose in anger and drew his sword.

My blade appeared as his was withdrawn from his scabbard and only then did he look at me and pale, but too late, my first riposte cut his arm and drew blood and an angry curse. My second lunge caught his damaged arm and after that I just taunted him with telling thrust after telling thrust as I weakened his defence. I knew he was skilled but that his sword arm was badly damaged, and although unfair, I pressed my advantage and finally gave the telling cut to his exposed throat after I had almost disarmed him. It might have looked impressive but an expert would realise I had deliberately killed the man.

Once his writhing on the floor had ceased, I asked the staff if they had felt threatened by the man and they confirmed he had brought terror to the inn and had severely injured two young men in a sword fight the previous day with much blood being shed.

When the Constable was summoned and came to the inn, the staff were fulsome in their praise of my actions in responding to the challenge and just having my sword to hand at the right moment.

After due deliberation, it was announced that I had acted entirely in self-defence and the matter was closed.

I suggested to the Constable that perhaps we should visit the room occupied by the deceased to ensure any money found there could be offset against the inn's charges. Pondering this briefly, he asked me to accompany him, together with the landlord, and the room was searched. Money was found and the bill settled but no other incriminating papers came to light and we returned downstairs. Quietly, the landlord thanked me for my consideration.

I then finished my breakfast and walked back to the overnight inn of my resting crew. Duncan apologised for breaking his bond but I accepted his word and made no other comment.

Three weeks later, we entered the outskirts of London, heading for Smithfield Market where we hoped to attract a top price for our cattle. Should I be fortunate enough to achieve a good price, I could pay off my men very quickly, send all our dogs home and see just what transpired after that.

Brokers men approached us as we neared the market, offering good prices for our herd but I decided to continue into the area to ensure I had the maximum offer available.

Haggling continued along the route until we neared Smithfield Market proper where I spotted a figure I had previously dealt with and he greeted me warmly. As usual, his starting price was derisory but we both knew the game and after much toing and froing we established a price of £12.10s.0d per head and I accepted his cash into my leather satchel.

We moved the herd to his instructions into a large holding area and parted with a handshake. My men accepted their monies and headed away from the market to seek cheap accommodation before drink and the long walk home. I told Dag, my dog, to "Go home" and hoped he was about to join the other dogs to lope home at an easy pace and retrace their downward journey.

Then it was into the unknown. I confess to being very frightened at this point. I was expecting trouble but no one knew how these braggards were taking down the drovers so with slow steps I secured my heavy satchel of money, but Dag had disobeyed me, he appeared by my side and I was touched by his loyalty but could not let him get involved in what I knew would be an ordeal.

Bending down to his ear level, I made it quite clear that he must "Go home now". He shook his head, looked very hard at me and then slunk off, breaking my heart to see him so miserable.

My cattle had sold for £12.10s.0d each, giving me £3,750.0s.0d and having paid the broker's fees and settled the wages for my men, I shouldered my leather satchel containing some £3,000 and strode towards the waiting ostlers and coaches.

Dirt and filth from the market added to the stench from the slaughtered cattle and I moved through the heaving morass of people to attract the attention of an ostler to find me a coach heading north. If this was going to work, now was the danger point and my fears rose as I was accosted by two large men who wished to convince me that not only had they the perfect coach and horses to hand, ready to head north but they could offer me a form of stirrup cup of warm wine to protect me from the cold.

Of course I drank heavily. We all do. I have done so all my life. It was when I detected a hint of something bitter in the wine that I hesitated. Some kind of drug...? Poison? I could have stopped myself right then but I could not. The country's security was depending on me.

I downed the wine and asked for more with a laugh. Another for the road...

I felt my knees go after the third. My vision swam and black closed in.

CHAPTER 11
RESCUED BY DAG

Shaken like a fish on the end of a line, I came out of a dazed state, staring at grass right next to my eyeball and feeling nauseous, sick, desperately thirsty and generally very poorly. Unable to believe my predicament, I attempted to use my hands but realised they were tied behind my back and shortly after that I realised my feet were also bound and I was freezing cold.

Suddenly the intense shaking that had woken me recommenced and this brought a moan of agony from my parched lips. Bile came to my mouth and I spat. Eyes now opening, I saw the grass moving across my vision as I was forcibly shaken, giving the awful sensation I was being dragged across a field.

Hot breath and a wet nose were the next sensations and with delight and huge relief, I realised that Dag, my huge wolfhound dog, had found me.

"Dag," I whispered hoarsely and was rewarded by a wet nose touching me and then the shaking torture recommenced.

Cursing loudly, I felt my bonds slacken very slightly and whispered louder, "Good dog," and the whole shaking business began again with renewed vigour.

For long periods, the dog stopped and panted by my side, trying to recover from the intense effort. We lay together but once rested, the dog attacked the bonds round my hands and after what seemed a lifetime, further movement was felt. Then we worked together to free the rope and with a sigh of relief I felt the slackening and the eventual release of first one hand then the other.

Exhausted, we both lay panting but then I was able to reach down to my boot top and was thankful to find my hidden dirk still in place. Once this was in my hand, it was short work to cut the ropes around my legs. I turned and rose on my knees and was violently sick, retching more foul bile and spittle but felt a little better as my breathing settled down.

I gave Dag a huge thankful hug of gratitude before using the dog as a support to rise to my feet. I remained still for a long while as the nauseous feeling subsided.

Upright and steady, now I was able to briefly recall my previous day's activity at Smithfield Market and the successful sale of all my cattle. But what had happened then? Of course... the coachmen and the welcome drink to a successful journey. Damnation! Now it became clear how the French rebels achieved their aim.

Collecting and replacing my dirk, we made slow progress out of the field and largely led by Dag we moved towards a nearby path.

I had no idea where I was and relied on the dog to guide me over obscure paths and fields for some distance, all without any food and no water anywhere.

We were at a very low ebb when I detected smoke rising above some trees a short distance away and we made slowly in that direction.

Gradually nearing the source of the smoke, exhausted from the long slow walk, we came to a small village and staggered through the few houses to the source of the smoke and a very considerable noise.

The ringing tones of a busy anvil signalled the village blacksmith hard at work in his roadside smithy and we slumped down exhausted by the entrance to get our breath back. It was at this moment the noise ceased and a huge leather apron swam in front of my bleary eyes as I lay with my back to the wall.

Kicking at my feet, the blacksmith said, "What the hell do you think you're doing?"

There was a long pause. Dag growled menacingly and the blacksmith looked a little closer at us.

I slowly looked up and said, "I'm a drover. I've used you to shoe some of my cattle and I'm knackered."

"Bloody hell, it's Jack, isn't it? I'm George Ward and that massive grey dog of yours gives you away. Wait and I'll get some small beer for you to drink. You look all in."

Moments later two leather tankards appeared but the smith gave the first one to Dag surprisingly and then I was offered a drink.

Drinking very slowly we took small sips and gradually

recovered. I couldn't help but ask why my dog was given a drink first.

The smith replied, "I saw the dog casting about late last night and thought it very unusual that you were not nearby. I watched as he hunted and hunted for a scent. That dog was relentless and covered the whole village before he moved off. His tongue was lolling out then and that was twelve hours ago. I think you have very nearly lost him with exhaustion, Jack, and you're not far away from that as well. What's happened?"

Later, over some very welcome bread and cheese, I had to think what to say and settled on the simple explanation that I had been drugged and robbed.

I could hardly tell him the truth.

CHAPTER 12
VISIT TO HOME OFFICE

George Ward, the blacksmith, listened to my story without interruption then looked again at me.

"So what happens now, Jack? How can I help you?"

I explained to George without giving too much away that I needed to go back and retrieve my lost money but perhaps he could assist. In my shoe I had placed one of the one pound notes I owned and on retrieving it I made my arrangements.

First and with great reluctance I insisted that Dag went home and this time he disappeared promptly on his long run home to Brough.

With George's help, I exchanged my heavy boots for workmen's shoes, removed my stockings and breeches in exchange for serge trousers, and my shirt and jacket were replaced by an artisan's rough woollen shirt and a hessian sack over my shoulders. My hat was replaced by a rough cloth cap and I looked just like any working man wanting employment. My dirk I placed in my belt under the loose shirt.

Next I shaved with George's strop razor leaving only the appearance of a large moustache on my face, thinned my hair and gathered the remaining strands in a ponytail hanging lightly down my neck.

George agreed to hold my clothes and sword in safe keeping and swore I looked like a down and out worker anxious for employment.

Shaking George's huge hand, I set off with a small pack of cheese and bread for sustenance and commenced walking back into London and to Smithfield Market but with an important visit to the Home Office first.

Not surprisingly, on arrival at the small office door, the Home Office staff refused at first to listen to me but eventually I prevailed and was summoned indoors where once again I entered the office of Mr Willoughby who appeared amused at my appearance.

Closing his door, we reviewed the situation to date and I gave him a very full account of my capture and escape plus the loss of my £3,000 which he took a careful note of. He confirmed my suspicions were correct. The spy in the Department had been revealed and he was currently enjoying time in the nearest gaol.

I explained my intention to get work in Smithfield Market and then follow the money when the next strike on a drover occurred. Mr Willoughby indicated I would be reimbursed for my recent loss at the hands of the thieves.

Mr Willoughby then went on to explain that, as

requested, a man had been identified, from the military, who would become my fellow traveller but he suggested the chosen officer might be an acquired taste and this proved accurate when the door swung open after a peremptory knock that announced the arrival of my support.

Swaggering in, the man ignored me and shook Willoughby's hand effusively, stating, "Get rid of the tramp and then bring me up to date, dear chap."

Perhaps I should have waited a little longer but anger caused me to kick the back of this man's knee and he dropped to the floor making mewing noises.

Mr Willoughby remained seated and silent whilst the man rose slowly and confronted me.

We were matched in height at about six feet and whilst I was fairly well muscled, my opponent was thin and scrawny by comparison, but his back hand swipe to my face carried a lot of force as I blocked it and punched low. He expertly dodged that and sent a kick to my body which would have caused serious injury if it had landed, and so in that confined office space, we fought like wild animals with a feral ferocity and intensity, both intent on giving severe injury to the other. Chairs were upended and papers strewn from the desk in our battle for supremacy.

In all the melee, Willoughby remained seated and was, apparently, an interested observer until in a very loud voice he shouted, "Cease."

We both dropped our fists and realised just how stupid we had been, made more apparent by Mr Willoughby's next cold remark. "I'm glad you have both met so cordially, but you will work together from this moment. May I introduce Lieutenant Hugh Sutcliffe, seconded from the Coldstream Guards to you, Squire Jack Rutherford of Brough in Westmorland."

For some reason I burst out laughing at this ridiculous situation and within moments Hugh Sutcliffe joined in and we stared aghast at the mess we had made of the chairs and fittings in that room. Controlling our mirth, we shook hands, quickly righted the furniture and apologised to Mr Willoughby.

Hugh whispered, "Fancy a beer?" to me to which I nodded.

Willoughby coughed into his clasped hands, demanding our attention and clarified matters. Hugh Sutcliffe was seconded to the Home Office to receive realistic field experience before a possible secondment abroad on His Majesty's Service. My role was to infiltrate the organisation of the Workers' Patriotic Revolt as quickly as possible. His was to protect my back.

It occurred to me at that moment there must have been one of our spies in the French Government office in London to have that information and the widespread implications of my role and its serious nature were confirmed.

A long lecture then commenced with details of the known activities of the WPR as they were called, together with the possible name of the prime instigator, a Monsieur Nicholas Bouchard. I had heard the name before, when the Earl and MP had first visited me, but it meant nothing to Hugh Sutcliffe at that time.

I stated it was my intention to visit Smithfield Market and obtain work there to view the methods and people involved in this uprising but that was not to be.

Our immediate task, we were told, was to take horses and travel quickly to Nottingham where Bouchard was spending money freely in the taverns on free beer and pies for those who wished to rise in rebellion against the government.

No time could be lost. We were dismissed after agreeing we could contact certain particular Constables who would pass information back to London.

We were escorted out of a small discrete shop door, away from any prying eyes, and made for the nearest tavern. Over a welcome pint of ale, we agreed Hugh would have to drastically change his appearance and alter his upper class accent which otherwise would be a distinct disadvantage.

CHAPTER 13
TO NOTTINGHAM

Work men's unkempt clothing would be needed and I suggested Hugh place a small pebble in his right shoe to encourage a limp. His cover story would be that he had suffered serious injury to one leg as an artillery man in the recent war and was partly deaf and unable to speak except in a guttural growl.

Next, we searched and found a form of pawn shop in the filthy part of the city and did some negotiating with the owner after we had locked his door to prevent others entering. He was concerned at first until we produced some small coin and after that it went smoothly although I doubted Hugh would ever see again his former smart clothing. Having changed our appearance to working class men, we unlocked the pawn shop door and stepped into the street as two former soldiers in appearance, down on our luck and looking for work but both with dirks in our belts hidden by our cheap woollen shirts and coats. The pebble idea seemed a good one but I had to remind Hugh it was his right foot!

The June day meant we still had light and after hiring cheap horses and saddles and collecting some food, we hid our paper money about our persons and made off for the long ride to Nottingham. We had a long hundred and forty mile ride ahead and rode till sunset where we found a tavern and took cheap lodgings with a meal and a rough straw bed in a barn. Nobody took any notice of us and after bread and cheese next morning, some of which we kept for midday, we set off with our leather flasks filled with clean water. Our horses had been stabled properly overnight and were fed, watered and chomping at the bit to be away on our early start.

Fifty miles we covered that day, helped by the long light nights and we repeated the previous day's routine each time we visited the bar for beer and a meal, Hugh displaying his inability to speak properly and attracting no attention.

It was during these long hot journeys that I took particular note of the passing cattle grazing in the fields and remarked to Hugh, while we could converse alone, that the area we were in held some excellent livestock in the fields and he responded with a firm discourse on cattle types and preferred breeds for different areas. He came from farming stock, I decided, but I knew nothing of Hugh's background only that he was a Lieutenant in a top British Regiment.

During the long ride, he seemed more than happy to elaborate.

•

"Jack, perhaps I can give you a little insight into my life to date. Yes, I know the land, but I come from a long line of military people and my parents always accepted my decision to join the army.

From Boarding School, I enlisted with the Guards as a trainee officer and left for service with the rank of Second Lieutenant where I was sent to France. I saw service across Europe and with the Coldstream Guards I was present at the battle of Waterloo particularly at Hougoumont. That was a stern and testing time but it gave me a keen interest in service to my country and a determination to succeed. It was at Waterloo that I distinguished myself and my promotion came as a result of that action. But war is brutal and savage and only the strict discipline of the Coldstream Guards and the raw courage of my men saw me through those dreadful days and nights of terror and distress.

It was during a period of training after that wonderful victory that my Commanding Officer called me aside and indicated I had been selected to apply for service with the government. I had made it known that my preference after my military career would be with the Diplomatic Corps but I had few expectations this high status would ever be made available to me.

All my hoped for ambitions suddenly became reality when I was selected for this dangerous mission to infiltrate the French Revolutionary agitators who have been fomenting dissent in England. My success in this task would give me credibility for any future government assignment and its importance was not lost on me.

We are an old Dorsetshire family and my elder brother will attain everything on my father's demise. It has always been my intention to make my own way to success and a career in the Government will enable me to rise to great rank if I am steadfast in my endeavours.

Surprise and almost indignation were my immediate reactions when I was taken into that dingy room to meet the burly character I was to assist in this assignment..."

•

We laughed and continued our discussions and it appeared Hugh's parents farmed in Dorset but not in a massive way and it was only on the advice and guidance from his uncle, a former Major in the Coldstream Guards that he was able to join that Regiment.

Swords had been his weapon of choice and I suspected he would be an aggressive and capable opponent. I intended to find out.

So we continued and two days later approached the environs of Nottingham.

At Wilford on the southern outskirts, we disposed of our hired horses, rightly believing that being mounted on horseback did not fit with our image. Nobody had questioned us so far because we looked somewhat fierce and former soldiers were not to be interfered with. That might not last however.

On foot again we reached the city in an hour and I reminded Hugh to replace the pebble in his right shoe if only to slow him down a little. Of course as a soldier he marched everywhere at a brisk pace whereas my pace matched my cattle. I suspected from conversation and what he had revealed so far that Hugh may be from the nobility and I meant to find out more eventually.

Our enquiries took us to the slum area of the city and the rough taverns where we made our beers last a long time as we listened to the conversation around the tables and sure enough, mention was made of free beer and pies the next night in a different tavern. We went straight there that evening and found rough bedding in a stable and the promise of free beer next day.

Wandering round the city the next day we agreed to split up that evening, leaving me to be 'enrolled' if possible into the WPR but leaving Hugh to tag along and join in separately.

Monsieur Bouchard himself attended that evening, speaking to a packed room full of honest and dishonest working men desperate for drink and particularly food for their hungry families.

Once the beer and food had been distributed, paid for with my damned money, I listened with growing horror to the diatribe spouting from the orator.

"You must understand," Bouchard announced to the room, "that England can no longer be under the rule of the aristocracy, but rather should spring to life as a free nation as we have achieved in France."

There was cheering, but mostly in appreciation for the pies.

"Your honest toil," he continued, raising his voice, "is not rewarded with decent wages or is rewarded with nothing at all. Your families live in penury whilst the aristocracy live in luxury and wealth, able to spend vast sums of money on fripparies, hunting, exclusive game parks and death to poachers." He looked around the room, gesturing wildly with his arms. "How much better will it be if we follow the excellent example of our French cousins who have disposed of their aristo's and now enjoy the rewards of that brutal exercise? How much better off will we all be if we join the Workers' Patriotic Revolt and show our resolve to change our lives forever?"

The cheers increased, the crowd beginning to take note, lured in by the thought of a better life. Who wouldn't be?

What Hugh thought of all this I dared not contemplate but fiery was the word for Bouchard's rhetoric and the crowd were swayed, there was no doubt about that.

I cheered along with the rest and made sure I was still clapping loudly when others had ceased which drew an admiring glance from Bouchard.

After further haranguing his audience, he stepped down to rapturous applause from his immediate entourage and apparent converts who were encouraged to sign a Declaration of Intent to receive the promised free pie.

Slowly and carefully, I moved forward in the crowd,

knowing that with my six foot height I would stand out, and sure enough Bouchard caught my eye and came over. He shook my hand and I congratulated him on his skilled oratory which he took on board with a condescending smile and invited me to sign the Letter of Intent. I deliberately played this down, insisting that as a former soldier but without work I felt nervous about the commitment. Sure enough, I got the full repertoire of facts and figures from his acolytes as he moved away and I allowed them to cajole me into signing, but not in my own name. How wonderful would my life be when once I joined the Party and was accepted then I would have a regular income, good food and lodgings and be able to use my skills as a soldier. We spoke at length, beer ran copiously down thirsty throats and the room became blue with tobacco smoke.

It was some time later that six burly Constables, armed with truncheons, arrived in the room, hitting shoulders and lashing out as they made for Bouchard to arrest him. Seeing my chance, I grabbed his arm and barged a way through the crowd, shielding him from sight as we fled with some of his men from the building by a side door I had noted. We all ran into a deserted street.

"What shall we do now?" cried the startled orator but I just bundled him into the darkness where we remained still for a long time as a search commenced but quickly ceased when angry customers chased the police away, having had their promised pies taken away from hungry stomachs.

That night Bouchard and his men slept in our barn on straw and early next morning they crept away but not before I had been given his heartfelt thanks. His men mentioned to me that they had nervously noticed Hugh's erratic behaviour as he acted his part but I explained about his terrible war experience which they accepted.

Strangely, there were copious numbers of pies offered for breakfast and I was quietly able to find out from the landlord where the source of his money came from to make so many items.

He hinted that the wealth dwelt in a smart inn some way out of town and I wandered over that afternoon to be seen eventually by Bouchard and invited to have a beer. After some desultory conversation, he asked if, as a capable former soldier, I would consider becoming part of his bodyguard.

The room was well furnished for a tavern and I suspected my money was being lavished on good living. Very annoying. Bouchard was at the head of the table, drinking wine, smoking a pipe and acting the generous host. He asked after my welfare and gradually steered the conversation round to his offer of a position as his guardian.

"I need a good man like you," he said, patting my arm. "The Movement needs good men like you. Join us."

I shook my head. "I'm looking for work on the land," I said, casually, working hard to be convincing. "My fighting days are over."

He looked incredulous. "You'd rather toil for the

bastard aristocracy than fight for your freedom. Come on, man. You've fought for your country. Fight now for your fellow countrymen. For your future."

He was good.

I took a drink of the damned good wine, being stubborn because it was paid for by my money – I would much have preferred a beer – while I seemed to be considering the offer.

"I don't know..." I said, reaching for a slice of pie.

Bouchard moved the plate closer to me. "Help us to help these people. Don't they deserve your sword now, more than ever?"

I hesitated.

"Dammit, man. How can I change your mind?" He smiled. "A regular wage weekly, food and a bed. What do you say?"

I glanced aside before looking back at him, leaning close and lowering my voice. "I have sworn an oath to protect my companion. I will not break that oath. I will not abandon him."

Bouchard's smile deepened as if he knew he was getting to me. "Then your companion also gets a regular wage weekly, food and a bed. I want men with me who are loyal to their word. What do you say?"

I nodded my head slowly, as if reluctant but as if swayed by that last offer.

And we were in.

I was asked to move premises to be nearby. I would be paid and I was to acquire swords for us both to protect

Bouchard and his immediate companions. He would pay me for both weapons.

For some time I had missed the familiar feel of a sword at my side and together Hugh and I quickly strode into the city. Reaching a suitable area, we enquired the whereabouts of an arms shop selling used weapons and an address was given.

Hugh and I looked the place over from a distance but saw only a smart clean façade and very little in the window display. Entering we were greeted somewhat carefully by the owner who appeared concerned at our scruffy appearance. I commenced a conversation with a display of money after which there was little problem. We secured two medium weight swords and scabbards and left promptly.

Our accommodation this time was a lean-to shed at the rear of the smart tavern which was basic but sufficient in the warm July weather.

Attending at 8am for our day's instructions as agreed, we were informed that nothing would happen today and we could relax. At my suggestion, we walked away to a quiet field hidden from the view of the tavern where I suggested we test our sword skills.

It quickly became apparent that Hugh was a master of the blade and we sparred long and hard to try and get an edge over each other. My long hours of practice at home seemed to be long past as I struggled to maintain my defence to a series of quick dashing attacks from my companion. With extreme concentration and a return of my inherent ability, I kept him at bay for twenty minutes when we both signalled an end and a well earned break.

Sitting together, breathless from exertion, he congratulated me on my ability. It appeared he had a formidable reputation with the sword whilst with the army and had won major tournaments.

For my part I was glad of the rest but we both resolved from that moment that we would constantly practise our swordsmanship as our lives might depend on it.

The next morning saw me report again and I learned we would leave that afternoon for Sheffield on horseback. I was asked if my companion and I could ride ahead and act as both guides and look out which was agreed.

CHAPTER 14
SHEFFIELD

Well ahead of the other mounted members of the Workers' Patriotic Revolt, we kept a wary eye out for the many thieves and former soldiers who roamed the countryside causing mayhem.

As a former soldier I could be expected to study the land ahead and anticipate danger. What I did not want to reveal was my full knowledge of the area from my droving activities and I hoped to take advantage of this by creating an impression of a professional soldier but using this to bolster my standing.

In a quiet moment I made Hugh aware of this, out of earshot of the others.

Constantly ranging forward and returning with details of the road ahead, I was able to insinuate myself into the WPR hierarchy over the long day's travel and we moved on reasonably dry dusty roads through the countryside. Sutton in Ashfield was reached in the afternoon and I suggested we all continue a little further.

As luck would have it, I stumbled on the small village of

Hardstoft and the Shoulder Inn which on enquiry could just accommodate all ten of us. Our horses were taken to be fed and watered and we enjoyed in my case a pint of beer. Hugh and some of the others tried a beer but Bouchard and the others insisted on wine which flowed freely.

Rooms were to be shared with Hugh and I outside again in a small wooden hut containing two straw palliasses and rough blankets, sufficient for our needs, and we returned to the main room of the inn for a simple evening meal of a meat pie and gravy.

We sat away from the main noisy body of men, giving Hugh a chance to quietly mutter his thoughts to me which seemed to involve a painful suffering for friend Bouchard for this fool's errand.

How Hugh kept his role up was beyond my belief and he had my admiration.

Retiring early, we had a peaceful night's rest and after more pie for our breakfast, we mounted again and made for Sheffield. I had hoped there would be some incident on the way to demonstrate my soldiering skill but the journey was untoward and we made the town that evening when again we found accommodation in the one slightly better tavern in the town centre.

Alarmingly, crowds had gathered outside from nine o'clock, anxious to see Bouchard and to be certain of a seat in whichever place he intended to address the populace, all of whom were distressingly thin and badly clothed. Some smaller children were barefoot and the women all wore long shawls over their heads and shoulders. All the talk was of a free pie and a beer.

Orders must have been sent ahead and at midday the appearance of a dray horse with many cloth-covered wicker baskets sent a loud shout of encouragement through the large crowd.

Bouchard appeared, waved to the crowd and begged them to follow him to a nearby well-known tavern, the Old Queen's Head. There he harangued them for one full hour, detailing the advantages of the French Revolution in removing the aristocracy and releasing land and money to the working man. Loud cheers and hurrahs greeted every pause in this diatribe and much free ale was distributed.

Once again, the forms came out to 'join' the Workers' Patriotic Revolt and only after a signature on the joining form was a hot pie made available. The signatures mounted quickly and the forms were placed in large wooden boxes, for what purpose I intended to find out.

By 3pm the crowd were in all senses eating out of Bouchard's hand and it was then he raised the awesome prospect of a massive march on London to attack the centres of power and start a rebellion. The crowd cheered their support for this action and they were promised that a date would be announced very shortly.

So, the pattern of the plot was emerging very clearly, rob the drovers and have a massive march on London to create mayhem and incite the masses to rebellion, all with free beer and pies. I needed to report this immediately.

Hugh and I left quickly, hopefully unnoticed and we

made our way with great care to the recently formed Police Station run by the Town Council. Once I was allowed, with reluctance, into the offices, I displayed my hand with my secret code and in a few words demanded to see the Chief Constable immediately.

For the next fifteen minutes I sat and waited until suddenly, with great ceremony I was whisked before a suitably uniformed person who announced he was the Chief of Police. He then dismissed all people and Constables in the room with a shout and wave of his hand.

Once seated again, he said, "Make your report please," whilst waiting to write my details down, dipping his pen constantly and nervously into the inkwell and angry at my deliberate brevity in reply.

I quickly explained my mission and responsibilities and asked he contact London soonest to update them on this potential grave rebellion. He was quickly aware of the danger to the government and assured me his report would be dispatched that evening in a letter taken by one of his officers direct to my contact at the Home Office. He asked after my welfare but I avoided answering and suggested I would prefer to leave quickly and unobtrusively.

Outside again by a quiet street door, I found Hugh, reported progress and we headed back to our duty.

Nobody had noticed our disappearance in the euphoric atmosphere of the meeting and we appeared on the periphery, thanking people for attending and generally making ourselves useful but with a watchful eye on Bouchard. Which was just as well as three most unsavoury characters had appeared, grabbed as many pies as they could and ran towards Bouchard, holding cudgels and demanding money. Both Hugh and I saw the disturbance and moved quickly across to confront the thieves, with our swords drawn and ready to use.

Our intervention was brutal and ugly. In seconds, one man had a slashed wrist from Hugh's lightning sword thrust then a second man was pierced through the thigh by my sword. The third man was pinned against a wall by two swords at his throat.

Bouchard's followers then gave the thieves a good beating before leaving to return to their base and we followed them back but not before a word of praise from the so called great man.

I was invited to join Bouchard for a pint and, once his men had passed out or called it a night, I took advantage to ask the Frenchman how he'd come to be in England.

He'd had enough ale by then to talk, maybe more than he should have...

CHAPTER 15
BOUCHARD

"Jaques," Bouchard said, raising his tankard and slurring his words, "I must admit that I was in somewhat of a compromising position when my tale begins…"

•

"Crashing blows on the door woke me from a drunken sleep and also disturbed the 'lady of the night' who slept next to me. Clasping her long coat over my naked body, I staggered to the door, removed the chair I had placed under the door handle and nervously opened it to be bowled over by two enormous gendarmes in full cry, "Attendez vous immediatement sil vous plez."

Staggering away from their garlic stench and fury, I knew immediately I was to be accused of being an 'Aristo' and could expect no mercy. Word had reached me through my contacts that the Prefect of Police, Guy Delavue intended to prosecute me for my Aristocratic background and my constant association with prostitutes.

Throwing the bed clothes over the police, and including the lady in the package, brought cries of further fury. In the melee I took to my heels, ran from the room and raced to the long flights of stairs down which I tumbled, clutching the cloak. I reached the apartment entrance to be stopped by another irate gendarme who overwhelmed me as I tripped on the stupid cloak.

All good things must come to an end, I supposed, and, Jaques, I knew my thieving, lecherous lifestyle of robbery and violence to the nobility would have to come to an end at some time.

During my thirty years of life to date, I have disappointed my parents, my late wife, various mistresses, government officials and their wives, politicians and particularly members of the various police forces with whom I have fought when resisting arrest.

Now after the usual thorough beating by the arresting officer and his colleagues, I was marched back upstairs and made to dress and I chose carefully. My black buckled shoes and long silk stockings were donned after my under garment and white pantaloon trousers. My silk shirt with the ruff was covered by my three quarter length light blue coat and I took my gentlemen's walking stick, of course.

Ignominiously, I was manacled to the largest brute of a gendarme and taken to Police Headquarters.

There I was thrown into a filthy cell and left for many hours without food or water, the usual softening process beloved of police in Paris.

I freely admit I was shaking with fear. Policeman and

Spymaster Guy Delavue was reported to be keen to make my acquaintance and his methods did not include a polite invitation. The guillotine was in frequent use despite the Revolution being some years ago. My father had suffered that fate and it appeared I was to be tried and killed in a similar way. Yes, I was scared.

Deep in the dungeon, cold and dark, I rested as best I could and awaited my fate.

During my eventful life I have enjoyed the privileges of a fairly wealthy upbringing but that was never exciting enough for me and I enjoyed gambling, drinking, the company of the wives of distant Ministers of the Government and thieving from all and sundry to fund my pastimes, all this from a very early age, I must admit.

I am also a swordsman and have enjoyed some successful duels with jilted cuckolded lovers and husbands, in fact I have a reputation as a fine man with a blade.

My suspicions are that this led to my incarceration and there was very little doubt I would be punished.

After probably two days and some long hours in my cell with bread and water offered infrequently, I was scared out of my wits and at a very low ebb.

Approaching heavy footsteps brought me slowly to my feet and I awaited my fate. Two gendarmes seized my arms and I was dragged up at least three flights of stairs and conducted along a series of long passages past rooms that became more ornate as we moved forward.

My arms ached from the firm grip on them and my

shoes had almost left my feet as I was thrust firmly forward until an imposing door was reached and I was released. It was suggested I try to improve my appearance. I was taken to a small room where a basin of water and a towel were offered which I used carefully. I brushed my clothing as best I could, rubbed my shoes on the back of my stockings and put my hands through my hair to improve my appearance. My guards watched me carefully.

Taken back into the ornate corridor, I was marched between guards and after loud knocking, the door was flung open and I was taken into an enormous room dominated by a stern figure who was busy writing behind an ornate desk.

No reaction came from my entry and the gendarmes placed me before my interrogator and quietly left the room.

A ticking clock intruded into the sudden silence and my body odours became more and more apparent as I stood in terror of my future.

"Take a seat before you fall over."

These words came slowly to my consciousness and I lowered myself into a nearby chair.

"You realise that I have enough information to send you to the guillotine without the need for a trial, eh?"

Prefect of Police for Paris, Guy Delavue was noted for his blunt speech and no nonsense approach and it was this august person who was addressing me. But why? I was a nothing. Yes, I had heard in prison that he wished to see me and that had been achieved. Whatever could be the reason for his involvement now? I waited. There was no other option.

"Speak up, Citizen Bouchard. What have you to say for yourself?"

What on earth could I say?

"Monsieur Delavue, any comment I make now will only dig my grave a little deeper, I fear, and I beg to remain silent."

"You are not going to any grave, at least not yet. I have a task for you to undertake in England but before you make any comment, I must add that it is dangerous, difficult, but entirely in the interests of our beloved France. Would you be willing to put your life at risk for your country in exchange for your freedom?"

This statement had me gasping for air. I was not to be killed immediately but could go on a mission for France and probably there be killed. I stared at the man for a long time and then nodded my head.

It was explained to me then just what was expected. England had long been a thorn in the side of France and conditions over the water were very confused. Many societies were being formed, promoting the rights and expected privileges for the masses. The English Aristocracy were feeling particularly threatened.

Our Revolutionary Republic felt then that this was the perfect moment for France to foment dissent in England and encourage a rebellion similar that in the Republic and of course if successful, France could invade and take England.

The breathtaking scale of the enterprise both surprised and excited me, as Guy Delavue knew it would.

So began the new career of moi, a down at heel semi-autocrat smoothly recruited into the bosom of French machinations against England.

Immediately, preparations were made for me to travel to England by coach as quickly as possible after a sensible method of communication was agreed and I was given a letter of introduction to the French Embassy in London from where my further instructions would come.

Leaving the confines of the Prefecture of Police, once again a free man, delight infused me and I stopped frequently on the Pont Marie bridge to admire the wonderful River Seine, then the Paris skyline, then later the stinking ordure filled streets of the so called famous city that I called home.

Money had been provided, letters of introduction issued and it was also made very clear that I was to be under constant surveillance. I was told to pack my bags carefully for a long trip away, leave nothing behind and dispose of all I didn't need.

This was accomplished with great speed as money lenders had already visited and relieved me of valuable francs already. A hasty early morning departure was successful and so my journey commenced.

Paris, Calais, Dover passed beneath my feet and I commenced the long coach ride to London with a feeling of accomplishment. I speak excellent English, having had a classical education but was nervous of general conversation and sat quietly in the crowded coaches and inns. I arrived in the city of London with a sense of awe at my task but a determination to succeed if only to save my neck.

After finding cheap lodgings from the meagre remaining funds I had been allocated, I made myself known at the French Consulate in a small side entrance, as directed and was escorted to a room where I was further briefed on my mission.

Money had to be acquired by any means and I was to gather émigrés and others to my cause and sow dissent. The suggestion was that I form a society to which like-minded people could be attracted, particularly the disaffected workers of the Midlands and the North who the Embassy knew were living in near starvation conditions.

Once my society was formed, I was to steal or rob to fund my activities and it was suggested that with enough money I could 'buy' new members by offering beer and food to new recruits.

My ultimate objective was to ensure a massive march on London to cause mayhem and foment rebellion. I was to remain remote from French Authorities and would be contacted by Embassy staff and code words were agreed.

Once outside again, I stood on the kerbside and watched in astonishment the sheer volume of carts, wagons, coaches, broughams and traps using the busy road and leaving foul evidence, as in Paris, of the horses passing.

Filthy, dirty and ragged urchins thronged the road edges, shouting and yelling. Dogs were everywhere and many rough men crowded the streets, all seeking paid labour.

I have to say, Jaques, that I felt a real sense of belonging in this squalid place and hurried to my meagre lodgings, anxious to start my search on the morrow for a killing ground to make money.

Within days I had gathered like-minded men to my cause with fiery speeches in low down areas of London using the public houses to expound my message. England is owned by the aristocracy who are using the working man to make their massive profits but giving little or nothing in return for honest labour. You agree, I know.

My message fell on welcoming ears and all the early signs indicated a good sound following but I needed money.

Wandering the filthy streets of London, I was drawn further and further into areas that the Embassy had warned me were dangerous in the extreme. London Docks and its surroundings I found most intimidating and the gang land culture made it clear I was not welcomed.

I attended the nearby racecourses but again found the criminal faction had all the possible loopholes and underhand tactics well under their control.

Wandering east, a change in the wind direction brought a foul stench to my nostrils and I moved cautiously in the general direction where I heard the bellowing of cattle in the distance. Moving nearer I came upon the great Smithfield Cattle Market where beasts are sold, slaughtered and prepared for the butchers' shops of London, all desperate for more and more fresh meat.

Here, perhaps was an opportunity to steal money in some way or another. Day after day I visited the market and became familiar with the workings of that vast area, the arrival of the cattle, the buyers and sellers arguing loudly, the swift despatch of the beasts and their carcasses being discarded in filthy sections of the area for picking over by urchins and then disposing of as best could be.

I have to say I was horrified at the whole process but by keen observation realised that the men who brought the beast to market were paid in cash!

Not only that, it was put in a satchel and the man took a coach ride away with his money.

I noted they always carried guns and swords and appeared a very hard target but anything is possible these days.

Considering the risks very carefully, I devised a plan. Talking to the ostlers and coach attendants, I realised that some were as ruthless a bunch of people I have ever met.

Men who would willingly take a bribe once I had bought them a fair amount of beer in their brief spells between horse changes became my new companions.

My plan was simple. I noted that coaches arrived on the outskirts of the market, disgorged their weary passengers and then the tired horses were changed for fresh ones.

Whilst this took place, potential travellers were gathered in the nearby inn and the various tavern maids, ostlers and grooms went about ensuring the coach was prepared and passengers identified.

At this point, drinks were offered to coach travellers before the long journey began and many took advantage of this offer.

It was at that very moment that there would be an opportunity to intervene if I could identify the correct procedure and make it work. After some hours of deliberation my plan emerged.

And what a plan! Over the past few months, many thousands of English pound notes were taken from the stupid drovers.

Those proceeds helped the Workers' Patriotic Revolt expand and grow its membership in towns like London, Sheffield and Nottingham to a considerable number of vociferous disaffected men and occasionally women who all wished to overthrow the British Government.

Meetings in the French Consulate have been conducted and I am being feted as a hero with every likelihood my scheme will bear fruit."

•

Bouchard guffawed, very pleased with himself and happy to brag to his new henchman. Me.

It had all been very interesting to listen to and I knew only too well how they managed to hoodwink the drovers, but I had a feeling there was more to it all…

CHAPTER 16
NOTTINGHAM

Next day we set off on horseback and the whole party was to return to Nottingham. Again, I was asked to ride ahead with Hugh and ensure that the passage of our small twelve man party was not threatened in any way.

Two days riding brought the outskirts of the city in sight and I determined to try to find out why we were returning here and not London.

Bouchard had only two other French men with him. The rest were the vociferous raging opportunists willing to resist any legitimate government if it fed their personal ambitions, and it was to some of these zealots that I directed my conversation at dinner that night.

It still infuriated me that all these meals and free pies and beers were being bought out of my stolen money and I had great difficulty not strangling one particularly infuriating individual.

Over dinner and beers that evening I chose one of the most outspoken of the hangers on and made conversation. He deemed it almost beneath his dignity to find himself in conversation with a former soldier but allowed that on this occasion I could benefit from his superior knowledge.

Taking a long drink from his very full glass of wine, he harangued me with words that silently infuriated me.

"Are you aware that this country of ours, that you have fought for, is in the hands of unscrupulous bankers who are controlled by the nobility and keeping England in serfdom," the buffoon burbled. "Do you not agree that the French Revolution has given that wonderful country the freedom to remove the aristocracy and create a system of government that we most sorely need here and now. Monsieur Bouchard has listened to my views on this matter and I have his ear on all the important matters that are being raised, indeed I have no doubt that I shall have a very senior position in the new government we will install once we overthrow the miserable beasts that are in charge at the moment." He seemed overly pleased with himself. "We have hundreds of supporters in the countryside just waiting to rise once we incite the masses. Our work in Sheffield and Nottingham has recruited the foot soldiers to lead the march on the capital. We cannot fail."

Now I could see, quite clearly, that this was no longer a small agitating minority but a well organised deliberate attempt to take over the country and my role had become more significant.

This man, dressed with a stylish neckerchief to match his blue velvet long jacket and breeches, was to my mind the last person on earth capable of management of any sort! I asked his name. It was Josiah Snyder, latterly of Essex and now attached to the staff of the Workers' Patriotic Revolt as Secretary.

Once I had bought him a further carafe of poor wine, he relaxed enough to give me more detail of the WPR plans.

I suggested it would be unwise for him to disclose too much information to a mere former soldier and now guard but he replied, "As you can probably not even read or write, you are fortunate to be receiving this wisdom from somebody who in later life you will revere."

By this time, I could hardly contain my anger and disgust at this condescending bastard but I stuck to my role and continued to appear impressed and congratulated him on his far sighted vision.

It was my mention of vision that made his eyes sparkle and more wine helped. He leaned towards me, tapped the side of his large nose in a gesture of inside knowledge and whispered, "We go to London, raise more money from our secret source and then the big march is arranged for October this autumn and don't you dare breathe a word of this conversation or you are dead."

Frankly I had heard enough, it was all I could do to control my urge to throttle the man but I had to keep to my role.

I accepted further drinks but made sure I remained alert and aware.

We partied late into the evening but as I made my excuses to say good night and went to leave the room,

I glanced back to see a member of the Bouchard party quickly move in to question Snyder. I would have to be careful.

Next morning after haranguing a crowded market place, we made arrangements to travel back to London.

Hugh had been informed of my findings and we both agreed that the information had to be with the Home Office as soon as possible but we were aware of a heightened security surrounding the whole gathering and we were both on our guard.

So began the long warm weary journey back to London which we accomplished in five days of steady riding.

During the ride, I noticed Bouchard held great store to a bound book that he consulted frequently, particularly as we approached a county boundary. Then he would flip through some pages, stare at the detail and then instruct an accomplice to carry letters.

I determined to view that book if possible and kept Bouchard under observation to see if an opportunity presented itself.

On the third day of our ride as we approached another county boundary, the book was again brought out of the saddle bag and carefully consulted. The accomplice selected this time was a large man but not quite sensible particularly after he had taken ale which he downed in large quantities.

My role was still to keep a little ahead of our group and ensure a safe passage so I engineered it that I moved well forward to be out of sight at the moment the messenger would come forward with his task.

A bottle of brandy just happened to be in my hands as the man appeared and all reason left him as I offered him a drink. We rode together for almost an hour before he slumped in the saddle and would have fallen had I not been beside him and saved his fall. In putting my hands round his body, I managed to slip the paper message out of his jerkin and glimpsed three names of prominent nobility who were to be informed that Bouchard was in the county and wished them to meet him and affirm their support for the coming uprising in London that they must attend.

We travelled on with me much more wary of the seriousness of the mission.

CHAPTER 17
LONDON

Once in London we were informed we must find our own lodgings but give our precise location to Mr Snyder who would inform us of our future duties. Hugh and I found a tavern but Snyder had insisted we be accompanied at all times by one of a number of his trusted allies who would monitor our movements.

We were both frustrated in any attempt to inform the Home Office of our startling news and we resolved to overcome this difficulty.

Hugh 'stole' a barrel of brandy, or so he hinted in his limited language whilst we were in company. In fact, he sneaked out and bought it but that didn't fit our plans.

That evening whilst he and I pretended to converse in his so called difficult language, our minder was treated to the sight of us both enjoying a glass of brandy from the small barrel we had tried to hide under the table cloth such as it was. Sure enough, a great interest was shown by this bruiser of a man and he hinted strongly how much he liked a drink too. I gave him a small glass but ensured he saw where we 'hid' the barrel and we then retired to our miserable rooms.

By midnight, when I checked, he was drunk and out to the world. In no time after that, I took off for the Home Office which I knew was manned night and day and after a long walk along dark roads and alleys, avoiding some of London's less scrupulous citizens of the night, I came in sight of the well hidden discreet entrance, knocked at the door and waited anxiously.

After what seemed a lifetime, a small window opened and I was asked my business. I had written my secret code on the palm of my right hand, as instructed, and without a word displayed this clearly to the window.

Bolts were heard being withdrawn and I was asked to enter slowly which I did, because behind the door stood two burly men, one with a drawn sword, the other with a pistol.

Asked to raise my arms above my head, I was frisked expertly and first my sword was removed then the dirk in my boot was taken, the latter with a frown of disapproval.

Swiftly after that, I was taken to a small office where a flustered clerk asked my business and became alarmed when I threatened to choke him if I didn't promptly see his superior officer on a matter of National Security and again quoted my secret number. He was out of that chair in seconds and I was asked to accompany him to a more secure room where I would be interrogated, which could be interesting and it was.

There was no mistaking my report was anticipated

eagerly and a very intense discussion took place with hastily assembled senior officers.

One gentleman took the lead, asking me in no uncertain terms, "Rutherford, what's your assessment of the situation and its potential for mayhem?"

"There is considerable support in the country for this movement against the government," I said bluntly. "The numbers massed on the ground are the dissatisfied, disheartened souls being recruited and encouraged from the desperately poor northern towns." I considered carefully what to say next, and pulled no punches. "I do believe," I said to this gathering of senior staff, "that the march and its prominence in the popular newspapers may be a way to disguise the true intention of the rebellious movement. More likely, I think the money being collected could further an attack on Parliament."

This statement was greeted with a cold silence.

"Where did that notion spring from, Rutherford?" was a point put to me by an imperious voice in the darkest part of the room.

I had to stay my temper. "As a man who has regularly survived in the most difficult environment of a drover," I said, seemingly more calm than I was feeling, "I am aware of subterfuge. This march and all its excitement would be the perfect foil for a determined attack elsewhere."

There was a long silence. "Thank you, Rutherford. You echo my own thoughts entirely, well done."

"What now?" someone else asked.

"Clearly the next major step will be the march itself,"

I said, "and if it gathers momentum then there would be blood on the streets of London. A contingency plan is needed, gentlemen, I'm sure you agree."

Another voice lacking any emotion at all said simply, "Noted. You can be assured that the government has that clearly in hand but we want constant information from you on the developing situation."

I explained my position in the WPR as a guard along with Hugh but said that our movements were being monitored and a further task was being suggested for me.

"I believe my commitment will be tested in some way," I said. "My gut feeling is that they'll ask me to rob a drover. I will try to keep you aware but it is extremely risky. Gentlemen, if this is the task requested of me, I will carry it out in my role as a zealot but I need an assurance that I will not be prosecuted afterwards."

My concern was that while manhandling an unfortunate drover, I would likely draw blood if the attack was to look realistic.

That imperious voice was the one to answer. "Rutherford, we have every confidence in your ability to act with reason."

This came as something of a surprise in view of my dark background that they were well aware of.

All this would be put in writing on the file, I was assured, but I was also reminded that I was acting for the government anyway.

I got up to leave with some foreboding.

Late as it was, the office was still very busy and I left by the same discreet exit and made my way out to our scruffy tavern after a reminder to take extreme care as my actions and dangerous undertaking was very much appreciated.

Through the smelly, badly lit streets I carefully made my way, thankful that I carried a sword to defend myself but my main difficulty was avoiding or dealing harshly with the endless urchins pestering for money.

Once back, I threw a small stone at our window and Hugh came down, unbolted the door and let me back into our room, passing the still sleeping guard on our way.

CHAPTER 18
ROBBERY AGAIN

Our morning ablutions over, we had intended to search the streets for a meal but were stopped from leaving by the very hung over bruiser.

"Wait here for Mr Snyder," he grumbled, which we did.

Snyder appeared shortly after and hustled me up to our dingy room, leaving Hugh to stare at the bruiser and gabble incoherently at him.

Snyder closed the door to our room and sat on the bed.

"I want you to come with me to Smithfield Cattle Market today," he said.

This was it.

This was where I would have to rob a selected cattle drover of his money before he was kidnapped and left almost naked out in the countryside probably to die. Snyder could not know how much of this I already knew, but here was the chance to clearly identify the ostlers who would carry out the kidnapping.

Snyder didn't give me any details but said that we would leave immediately for the long walk to Smithfield, adding,

"You'll be given a leather satchel with a lock on it and you'll bring that back to these very lodgings without delay. Do you understand?"

Snyder was unaware that I was known in a very limited way in the Smithfield Cattle Market from my visits over the last three years and I was very nervous I would be recognised.

My rough clothing would help and a different hat was now used but my height at six feet made me stand out anyway and a more subtle approach had to be made. Nor could I discuss this with Snyder without giving him suspicions about my bone fides as a former soldier.

As we were about to leave, I hesitated.

"What is it, man?" Synder snapped.

"My army service ended somewhat disastrously," I admitted. "I struck an officer and went AWOL. The army are very keen to have me back in their clutches which makes the venture to the cattle market a risky move unless I can disguise myself."

He regarded me awkwardly for a moment and I thought I might have given myself away but he then nodded. "I'll get someone to give you a hat, large enough to cover your ugly face. That should do it."

And so with a vagrant's hat and my filthy dusty coat, I made my way, led by Snyder, to the great cattle market at Smithfield.

No sword was allowed and my dirk still nestled in my boot top as we trudged through filth, dirt, grime and the smoke filled streets to our destination.

I had to behave as though the market was a strange event for me but it seemed Snyder had been before and he led us to the very tavern from which I had been kidnapped. Although I had taken precautions and was now wearing the over-sized hat, it seemed inevitable that I would be recognised. But no, fresh faced ostlers and coachmen jostled and shouted as coaches were emptied, horses changed and new passengers were collected and despatched constantly.

Drawing me to one side, Snyder indicated a rotund person carrying a large satchel who approached the tavern and asked for a coach to Wales. Immediately two ostlers separated from the crowd and asked the gentlemen to join them in the tavern to pay for his coach and arrange for his place on board.

Pushing me forward, Snyder indicated I join the group and then he just disappeared. Once I was in the tavern, I allowed my eyes to become used to the dark and took my bearings. The two ostlers had taken a table and were asking questions of the drover, where in Wales he wanted to go, north, south or centre, and was he needing the carriage trip immediately or would he need accommodation, all the while plying him with generous portions of ale.

On my entrance, they beckoned me over to sit at the table but out of the drover's line of sight and signalled I should remain silent.

After fifteen minutes of this conversation, they must have slipped him the spiked ale and our 'drunken' drover passed out completely, at which they gave me his bulging satchel and watched as I transferred the many paper notes into my own satchel and was about to lock it but not before they had demanded their 'fee' of £10.0s.0d which I paid and then safely locked the money away.

"Don't I know you, Mister?" was the unwelcome response after I handed them their cut of the money. "I'm sure I've seen you round here before and you're not local with that accent."

"If you want to make a fuss, let's do it in here and now," I said, quietly drawing my dirk out of my boot and watching them carefully. "I'm retired from the army if you know what I mean and I don't take to people asking questions so which one first? You?"

The biggest of the two rose from his chair and then broke it in his fall as I smashed my boot into his groin. The second man was slow and I had my dirk to his throat in an instant and he remained very still as his mate thrashed about with the broken chair.

Pushing the second man back in his chair, I suggested they stay inside a little longer as I fastened his hands to the furniture with a piece of twine from my pocket. Then taking the satchel, I left to watch from the side.

Eventually a horse and cart appeared, the drugged drover was thrown in the cart and a canvas placed over him. I looked carefully at the two men doing the manhandling and committed their faces to memory. After that, I strolled slowly through the bustling throng of cows, men, dung and slaughtered beasts, carefully making my way back and retracing my journey to our lodgings.

Had any of the crowd of desperate hungry filthy men and women known just how much my satchel held, my minutes of life would be very short, but dressed suitably I blended in and made it safely back to find Hugh looking out for me and Snyder demanding my satchel and its contents.

CHAPTER 19
ATTACK ON POLICE

Neither Hugh nor I had any inkling of just how much money had been stolen but the amount gave great joy to Snyder and his next announcement took us completely by surprise, an attack on the police in London.

It seemed Bouchard was so pleased with the amount collected, he felt the moment had come to test the resolve of the police and cause a deliberate riot.

Our role, it appeared, was to visit the slums of the East End and the Dockland area and recruit enough dissatisfied men to encourage them to march through the streets and challenge the police.

We would be part of a group of 'patriots' who would buy beer and offer pies again as long as the hungry men signed the WPR papers.

We arrived in the East End of London, having travelled on the top of stagecoaches at the cheapest rates and we made our way through the crowded filthy streets to our very poor tavern.

Next day we were summoned early, given small beer

and gruel then took horses and carts laden with freshly baked pies and entered the dingy streets of Docklands. The response was frighteningly successful, word quickly spread, beer was consumed in quantity and warm pies were given once the papers to join the WPR were signed.

Urchins crowded nearby, squabbling and fighting among themselves as some pies came to their grimy hands to be devoured instantly.

Then Bouchard chose an outdoor open space and started his well rehearsed harangue about the glories of France and its wonderful Liberty, Egalite, Fraternite. This was largely lost on the gathering crowds but when the suggestion came that they take on the police who were protecting the governing classes, this went straight to the mob's conscious.

In a very short time, the crowd, roaring with drunken fervour, headed for the nearest Police Station and laid siege to it.

Hugh managed to disappear at my suggestion and ran when out of sight to the next Police Station to sound the alarm and bring reinforcements which they did.

I was in the thick of it, at Bouchard's side and making sure to protect him. The fighting was fierce, and as I clocked the increased police presence, I made sure to bundle Bouchard aside and encourage his cronies to slip away with us.

I could see behind us that Hugh's police reinforcements arrived before any serious damage occurred and within the hour a lot of bruised shoulders and sore heads could be seen in the area and for many days afterwards. But significantly there were no arrests made to make martyrs to the cause.

.

CHAPTER 20
MASSIVE MARCH
PLANNING

Once back at our lodgings, Bouchard declared his delight with the outcome and announced that the time had come for a massive march to be arranged.

We would all return to the northern cities of Sheffield and Nottingham, recruit followers to the cause and with funds available make the march on London and bring the city to a standstill.

Further, the marchers would be encouraged to attack the police with a vengeance and then move to the Houses of Parliament to wreck as much of that building as possible before setting fire to the traditional centres of power in England.

Bouchard made it abundantly clear that overthrowing the government was at the heart of his ambitious plan and we, as his loyal followers, would be bound to him by oath and from now on we must not mingle with others, on pain of death, remaining always in his sight or that of his immediate cronies.

Hugh and I realised that this was the moment when we desperately needed to warn the authorities and would be helpless to do so.

Gathering horses for all the followers, we set off on what was hoped to be the final visit to those northern cities whose angry hordes, already inflamed with talk of insurrection, would rise, with food and drink available, and march to their possible doom.

Hugh's role as a stuttering mute and our close proximity to the other followers of Bouchard made it extremely hard for us to communicate. Left to my thoughts, I devised a plan to warn the authorities that was fraught with danger of course but possibly workable.

Snyder now carried the satchel containing the stolen money and from its bulge I could imagine it held a considerable sum, enough to cause angry men to leave their wives and families and march on the government in a drunken state and cause mayhem.

It was late September and the fields we passed held newly made straw ricks, showing that the harvest had been made and the granaries filled. Men in the fields with horses and carts stopped briefly and waved as we trod past, little realising the significance of the gathering, and under close watch I could pass no message as we rode through towns and villages where occasionally the local Constable appeared to watch our movements but of course was not alarmed.

My suspicion was that I was being closely watched at all times and something in my demeanour or attitude must have made Snyder wary of my enthusiasm for the cause. Testing this theory and pretending a stone in my horse's shoe, I halted, signalling I would catch up once the matter was dealt with, but Bouchard and one other thug stayed with me as I used my dirk to 'remove' the offending stone and remount. Clear evidence that I was under surveillance.

Long days in the saddle, rough accommodation in taverns and inns and being watched at all times made that journey seem interminable and it was with some relief we reached Sheffield and took our previous lodgings.

Twice on the journey I was provoked into fighting after beer was spilled on my clothing and my food was disturbed. Each time I bettered the assailants but it was obvious now that my position was being questioned.

CHAPTER 21
SHEFFIELD MASS MARCH

Within one day of our arrival, arrangements had been made for a mass gathering in the city and again we met at the Old Queen's Head tavern which had a large space nearby.

Pies were displayed on a cart travelling round the city and hordes of men, women and children followed until they all arrived at the tavern.

Workers' Patriotic Revolt banners were revealed, a secret kept from me, beneath which those who had WPR papers were given a pie and the men offered a drink from the huge barrels of ale that had appeared outside the tavern. Chaos ensued, as was to be expected. Food was passed from hand to hand, beer was flowing in great quantity and my task was to ensure each man who had signed up became intoxicated and this happened very quickly.

Bouchard chose his moment perfectly, stood on a beer barrel and with my and others help drew the attention of the crowd.

His half hour speech started low key, but rose to a crescendo as he outlined the terrible forces at work to keep the people under subjugation. Workers' rights, outrageous food prices, long working hours for a pittance of pay whilst the gentry lived the high life of languor and idleness without a care for their fellow man.

It was powerful stuff. Pausing for effect after his thunderous oratory, he asked the crowd, "What are you going to do about it? Will you remain downtrodden all your lives or are you willing to join me in a grand march? If I give you pies and beer tomorrow, will you pledge to follow me in a massive Grand March to London and demand our rights to a better future and well paid work?"

The noise was deafening. The crowd loved it and cheered each sentence.

As I hoped, the police arrived and after some fierce arguments, they set about trying to clear the square but fights started.

Truncheons drawn, the police charged the main centre of commotion and I joined in quickly after a wink to Hugh who stood nearby and was now aware of my plan.

In moments I was bellowing for people to follow me and formed up to attack the many police on the scene. Fists flew, truncheons beat down and I made sure I received a good number of blows before a particularly large Sergeant knocked me down and handed me back to a colleague who snapped a handcuff on my wrists. I was bundled back and held on the ground, immobile.

Two hours after the outbreak of fighting, the police

had partial control of the streets and retired back to their secure building, hauling me and ten other desperadoes to be dealt with severely in the cells.

There was little or no finesse once we were in the Police Headquarters. We were taken to the cells and beaten with truncheons whilst wearing handcuffs. Nobody was spared and when they had finished, we were left in a cold damp cell made for four people and now containing eleven aching bodies with no place to lie down or rest our aching bones.

At some point, I had to get the attention of a Sergeant and display my secret sign but this had to be done out of sight of my fellow prisoners, some of whom were part of the WPR bullies I had previously had dealings with. They no longer considered me a threat as I had absorbed the same amount of punishment as they had but they were a threat to me.

With nothing to lose, I started banging the cell bars and demanding water and I carried on like this for more than an hour when a policeman came, demanding to know what the commotion was.

I beckoned him over, winked at him in a conspiratorial way and grabbed him by the throat as he leant over, and banged his head on the bars.

Within seconds, the cell was alive with shouting, screaming prisoners. Reinforcements came and rescued their colleague who pointed to me and demanded I be released into his personal custody for ten minutes.

To my surprise, this was granted. I was removed from

the noisy cell and the beating started as soon as I came within range of the boots of my so called custodian. Not once in the long walk to the upper part of the building did my tormentor cease in his blows but as we were moving, I was being hustled along by two of his burly shift members and I was able to tolerate or avoid some of the punishment, but I was out of earshot of my companions at last.

Once in a form of office, I let out a fierce war cry from my wild youth and they stopped in their tracks.

Thankfully, a Sergeant appeared, asking what the hullabaloo was.

I caught his eye and rather cheekily asked if I could have a word with him. But I addressed him in a cultured voice similar to that used to my servants and the man looked at me closely, shook his head and walked away, to my distress. But he shouted over his shoulder, "In my room without blood showing in two minutes," and he walked off.

Once in the Sergeant's office, he bade me stand and explain why I had made such a request. Slowly and without interruption, he heard my story and took brief notes. Alarm showed on his face when I explained both the gravity of the proposed march on London and the massive numbers involved. I then gave him my discreet number which brought him to immediate action. He left the room and returned very quickly with an authoritative man who was the Chief Constable.

Once he had heard my tale and my confirmation of

my discreet number, the Sergeant was dismissed and then the Chief Constable agreed that although this sounded serious, he was not convinced that there were sufficient grounds to alert the Home Office but he would note my concerns in his next monthly report.

I was now free to go.

Outside, Hugh and Snyder were waiting for me, the latter taking great pains to enquire why I had been released but the rest of his gang of ruffians would be released with a fine the next day.

In my considered opinion, the Chief Constable had made the most dreadful mistake in releasing me before the others and had brought Snyder to realise I may be different to his other villains.

I had to get Hugh on his own and task him with walking or riding to London, visiting the Home Office and warning them that this Rebellious March was gathering pace very quickly and there would be bloodshed if and when it reached London.

We scurried away from the Police Station and made our way back to the tavern we used, but all the way Snyder questioned me repeatedly about why I was allowed out, and despite my bruises and cuts and a black eye, he remained extremely suspicious of me.

For my part, I explained that I had tricked a Constable into coming too close to the bars of the cell and had tried to choke him, which brought a lot of his colleagues to his assistance where I was taken from the cells and severely beaten which only stopped when a Sergeant intervened and suggested I was allowed to leave as the Magistrate may question why I was bleeding so much. It sounded good to me but failed to impress Snyder at all.

Nearing our tavern, Snyder went ahead and I took the moment to urgently suggest to Hugh that he leave at once with any money I had. He had to reach London as quickly as possible and alert the authorities of the dire consequences of delayed action. In my opinion, there would be in excess of 1,000 people on this March.

He agreed, took some of my remaining money and strode off on his dangerous errand.

From that moment onwards, I was under close attention from all senior members of the WPR.

Hugh's absence was mentioned to me and I suggested he had family issues which must be attended to but my lame excuse was noted and frowned upon.

My revulsion of the methods being used by Msr Bouchard left me more than angry with the position I was placed in.

CHAPTER 22
RUMOURS

Next day Bouchard and many of his cut throat French murderers disappeared from the tavern. Snyder was giving the instructions and appeared to be in charge.

Immediately becoming suspicious, I made some careful enquiries and came to the reluctant conclusion that the bulging satchel I had seen contained far more money than I had imagined.

But of far more concern to me was learning quietly that the hasty departure of the chief agitators was to a special meeting in London to coordinate the attacks on the seat of government. Here was the very reason for my becoming involved and I was in Sheffield and not London.

A rapid escape from here was essential. I slipped into the tavern unseen, collected my meagre belongings, girded on my sword, prepared my pistol with fresh powder, set the flintlock on safe and left the building. But how to disappear silently and reach London in a short time?

It was nearing noon. Food would be served and my

absence noted but that might work in my favour. If I could find a spot and remain hidden, the hue and cry would assume I had gone south and many of the gathered scoundrels would set off in wild pursuit. By evening it would be more opportune to move away under cover of darkness but that would be some time yet.

I had previously found a tumbledown old single storey hovel with thorns and brambles covering it and had earmarked it in case I needed a hideout. It was here, within sight of the tavern where we had lodged, that I made my way, carefully covering my tracks and entering the place without disturbing the surrounding greenery. Then I waited and it was a long wait but worth it. The noise and disturbance my absence created gave me reason to fear for my life as the reward for my death or capture was roundly shouted to the gathering mob by an irate Snyder.

Sheffield to London is an awesome hundred and seventy mile journey just walking, and could take days whereas I suspected Bouchard and his crew of political rebels would travel by coach. So I would do the same. But I would walk due east and connect with the Great North Road where, with good luck, I would find a stagecoach heading south and use the last of my money to purchase a ride.

First I had to escape and this I did once darkness fell. It was not easy and twice I thought I had been spotted but with my dark clothing I blended into the darkest parts and crept away. My route was to go for the roads leading through Worksop and reach the Great North Road a further five miles from there, a distance I mentally guessed at about twenty-five miles. Fit as I am and familiar with this area and its roads, it would be daylight as I neared Worksop and I was a wanted man with a price on my head.

So it was that by pushing my body to its very extreme, I reached the outskirts of Worksop and despite being heavily armed, I attracted little or no attention from passersby. My hope was to come across a wagon and horses to ease my aching legs but nothing moved in the area. Shortly I became anxious for somewhere to sleep and to eat and drink. A rude tavern appeared and looked extremely unkempt but in my guise as a down at heel drover it suited me just fine. The stench of stale beer and unwashed bodies was almost too much for me but a few pence saw me with a room for the day and a meal and small beer before I found my bed which was so dirty I lay fully clothed and slept but not before I placed a chair under the door to prevent it opening.

Having slept soundly, I rose at 6pm, washed in the basin and replaced my smock and jerkin and my sword. The pistol remained hidden but handy.

My evening meal was a meat pie with boiled potatoes and a small beer. There were some interesting characters in the room but I ignored them, finished my meal and paid the landlord for my dues but I made no mention of the fact that I would be gone just as darkness fell.

Away from the tavern, I walked briskly to rid myself of

the cloying stench and by 11pm I neared the Great North Road and sat by the wayside, awaiting my opportunity for a stagecoach. It was my hope that one of the stages for horse changes would be nearby and Ranby was the nearest village from my recollections of this part of the Great North Road, so to Ranby I walked.

At that time of night, anybody on the roads was a suspect and I tread warily, hoping to hear a coach approaching and possibly stopping but to no avail. I sat under a tree on the road side and fell asleep as only a drover can but a noise woke me at about 6am and a coach appeared. I threw myself into its path and was greatly relieved as it slowed to a walk.

The business end of a huge blunderbuss gun reared up at me, its mouth looking like a cave entrance. I was told to put my hands up by a very irate coachman. Our conversation was brief. He had no passengers and, yes, I could ride with him, for a fee paid up front and we could proceed to the next stage stop where he was going no further. I was not allowed in the plush interior but was placed on the roof where it was extremely cold.

At the next stage stop, I felt a little more at ease. The coaches stopped regularly in my home town of Brough and I hoped to see at least one friendly face among the many persons who were changing horses, shouting at passengers and moving vast amounts of luggage from coach to coach.

By watching and listening, I learnt that a suitable fast coach was London bound and the young urchin I consulted took me to the coachman and I secured my passage but again on the damned roof.

London bound within the half hour, I suffered the agonies of the damned and silently cursed Bouchard and many others to while away the time. The next stop was Newark, then Grantham, then Stamford and that was a long nine hours so I was glad to leave the coach briefly and freshen up in the nearby tavern. My coach allowed thirty minutes for toilets and food, then with a change of horses was ready to leave.

I counted my dwindling money, tidied up my appearance and paid the excess coin to travel in the interior of the coach because I had noticed there were no passengers going further, only me. Some negotiation took place with a hint of violence on my part which convinced the coachman I was best out of his way and so began the next trying part of the journey but in the comparative opulence of the closed upholstered seats, I fell fast asleep to be woken, after six hours by an astonished coachman who claimed, "Nobody sleeps in a moving coach, young man."

So I continued, night and day, resting when I could, eating, toileting and sleeping until we reached London in two days. I was weary beyond words and I still had to get my message to the Home Office where doubtless there would be watchers hoping to stop me.

Arriving in London, I chose to wait until darkness to approach the Home Office building housing the officers to whom I was to report.

Nearing the address, I approached with extreme caution, ever conscious of being prevented from giving my report which would wreck the dreams of the Workers' Patriotic Revolt.

I remained in the shadow of a nearby building and watched the discreet entrance and the surrounding buildings. My patience paid off. Movement came from a nearby alleyway and slowly two burly figures could be seen, with cudgels, watching and waiting. It surprised me that this activity could be taking place so very near to the heart of English Intelligence gathering and I became concerned at this lack of security.

There was now little chance of my entering the building without being noticed so I remained hidden and considered my options. For a further thirty minutes, I remained totally still and watched the two assassins and became convinced they were the only two watchers.

Slowly doubling back into the gloom behind me, I thanked my lucky stars I had taken precautions then I back tracked and circled.

The assassins had rather foolishly remained together at the narrow end of an alleyway and I suspected it would be possible to creep up on them from behind and remove them from the equation.

I collected some small pebbles into my pocket, drew my heavy cudgel and over the next long minutes I stalked these killers with all the cunning at my disposal. It seemed as though hours had passed before I was low to the ground crawling towards my target. Rising to my feet not five feet behind them I threw a small pebble over their heads to land on the ground in front of them.

"Attendez," whispered one man and he peered round the corner, brandishing a knife.

My first blow to his colleague dropped him unconscious to the ground and I leapt at his companion, swung the heavy cudgel into his face and he screamed as he fell. A second blow silenced him too.

Not surprisingly, this brought people into the street but I quickly hauled one man to the door of the Home Office which opened, someone grabbing my assailant, and I then returned, hauled the second unconscious man into the building and closed the door behind me.

"Very well done, Mr Rutherford. We wondered how you would deal with that matter."

It transpired that the whole building was aware of the killers but had not quite worked out how to deal with them when I was spotted and it was decided to leave it to me.

This information I was given over a cup of tea whilst being questioned by Mr Willoughby whom I had met previously with Hugh Sinclair.

I asked after Hugh's well being but was met with silence.

My information on the activities of the Workers' Patriotic Revolt was alarming to say the least and my suggestion that the march from the north was a diversionary tactic was met with extreme doubt at first and then considerable concern.

Again I asked after Hugh but was met with silence.

CHAPTER 23
HUGH

I was given a place to stay and it was the next morning that Hugh surprised me by climbing in through the window, looking much the worse for wear but alive and well.

Before going down for breakfast, he regaled me with the adventures he'd had since leaving me in Sheffield. As Hugh began...

•

"From Sheffield to London is a long one hundred and eighty miles and I knew I would have to walk the entire distance.

That, as a soldier, should not have caused me any problems particularly as I could remove the blasted stone from my right shoe and walk properly again. Fifteen miles a day is possible with good food and plenty of water but I could not rely on inns and hostelries as I was certain to be trailed all the way.

In that time the Rebellion could have reached

Nottingham on horseback and encouraged a further crowd to join the march. Time was of the essence.

I was taking with me your suggestion, Jack, to deploy the military outside the city and divert the marchers into a suitable large estate where they could be offered soup and food if they agreed to disband. Under military rifles that could well happen and would prevent bloodshed. The Peterloo Incident in Manchester was still raw on the public's nerves.

Walking quickly, hiding in any location I could find, I used your money for food, small beer and rough accommodation for three days and made some fifty five miles by my rough calculation.

Desperate times require firm resolution. I needed a horse or a coach. I stole my first horse near Northampton on my fourth day of travel. It was just getting dark at about 7pm when I came across a lively party of farmers enjoying talk of a good harvest and drinking good ale.

Their loud voices and laughter gave me the idea that their horses would be tethered nearby and sure enough I found them and chose very carefully. I led my horse away from the rest, nuzzled his nose into my jacket and whispered to him as we walked away on the grassy verge to avoid noise from his shod feet.

Half a mile further and despite being tired, I mounted the horse and rode well into the night before I stopped and used a hay barn to feed the horse, water him and find rest for myself.

That day I travelled approximately twenty miles. The

poor horse was weary and I let him go to find his way home. The next forty-five miles were extremely difficult. Scrounging a lift on an empty stagecoach was a blessing but that landed me on the northern edge of the city in the Edgeware area and I started walking, making good progress. By this time I had abandoned my deaf mute role and took to the road as a soldier, marching quickly to cover the final twelve miles to the Home Office to give my report.

Traffic flowed steadily through the crowded streets as I neared the city, Hansom cabs, horses pulling carts of bricks and timber mixing with members of the public hurrying about their business and the occasional Brougham invariably with a pretty girl and her beau being shown the sights by the driver. All this and barrows being used and children playing gave the roads their busy feel.

Knowing the French assassins were probably ahead of me put all my senses on full alert.

The impression we'd gained was that we were now expendable to these Revolutionaries and the sooner the better. No quarter would be shown in the event of a confrontation.

I walked quickly on through the increasing traffic aware of the disparity between the poor bedraggled beggars and urchins crowding the edges of the street and the rich trappings of the carriages whisking 'the fancy' to their destinations in style. That had been my world until I joined my Regiment and saw battle and that realisation brought a long period of reflection as I strode to my destination.

That brief period of introspection nearly cost me my life. I had ceased my vigilance.

A loud "Arretez vous" immediately put me on alert. Looking back, I saw two of Bouchard's assassins, waving swords and running towards me. I broke into a fast run and kept up the pace but they gained on me steadily. Passing traffic lurched away from these killers but one Brougham kept pace with them and then the horse broke into a good gallop and passed them by, making for me.

As the carriage drew alongside, a very pretty girl nonchalantly waved her fan and said loudly, "You'd better jump in, dear," which I did with haste and watched my assailants disappear in the enveloping traffic.

"It is you, Hugh, isn't it?" she said in a sweet voice that was strangely familiar. "I hardly recognised you with that strange garb but your face and hair remain clear in my mind."

I was astounded. I was in the company of the rather wild and dashing Lady Arabella Forsythe who, when last heard of before I went to war had successfully sailed a yacht out of Poole Harbour, on her own in heavy weather and saved a dog that had been washed out to sea.

How she had remembered my name I couldn't imagine but right now I blessed her intervention and asked her to take me immediately to the Home Office.

She refused and told the driver to continue until I gripped her arm, told her this was very serious and to clearly instruct the driver and make haste.

She did this and then smacked me on the face for

hurting her arm. We got on well after that and I obtained her address before leaping out and making my way here, old chap."

•

I must admit, I laughed at Hugh's telling of his escapades despite the severity of our circumstances. We had breakfast and made our way back to the Home Office.

Our meeting with Mr Willoughby took place in an office that included the Home Secretary and another person who was unnamed. A file marked Top Secret was placed prominently in front of him and he called for complete silence.

"What I am about to disclose to you both," Willoughby said, "has been declared Top Secret by the government and the presence of the Home Secretary indicates the serious nature of this matter. Under no circumstances will you discuss this matter outside of this room."

He then went on to explain that in 1820 there had been an uprising against the government known as the Cato Street Conspiracy where disaffected persons met at that location and intended to murder the Prime Minister, Lord Liverpool, and his Cabinet whilst they dined at Lord Harrowby's house. A spy within the group ensured that the would-be assassins were caught but a Bow Street Runner was killed in the melee.

"There is a distinct possibility," he continued, "that these Workers' Patriotic Revolt intend to harm the government with a lightning raid on the House of Commons supported silently by the French Revolution faction. Both you, Rutherford, and you, Sinclair, are familiar with sword play and your unwritten instruction from this meeting is to remove this threat by whatever means possible. Our investigations suggest that history is repeating itself and the conspirators are meeting at Covent Garden's White Lion Inn as we speak. You will go there, armed, and gain entry. Arrest the traitors or deal with them as you see fit."

Willoughby paused, looking at us both to gauge our reaction.

Satisfied, he then said, "You are both known to the underlings guarding the tavern and might easily slip their guard but be under no illusions, there are assassins from France in that building just awaiting a chance to shed English blood. If and when you are inside, you will create as much confusion as possible in the hope that some of these persons will flee and once you are both indoors, we will have the building quickly surrounded by armed forces."

Willoughby stood then. "Go and God speed your endeavours."

CHAPTER 24
THE KILLING ROOM

Outside again, Hugh and I looked at each other in blank amazement. We were both hardened to possible death and injury, he as a serving officer of the Guards and me with my background as a drover but never had we contemplated being thrust into armed conflict against at least possibly seven bodies, all on a serious mission.

We paused in our travel to Covent Garden to assess the risks we were about to face. Bouchard always had three men at his beck and call plus two assassins brought in from France, so at least five people to deal with, probably more plus Bouchard and Snyder.

As Hugh remarked, "Whatever plan we make will change once we start our small warfare but let's consider what we can do."

I recalled visiting this tavern at the end of a long drove and from my recollection there was always a large fire in the bar where all gathered.

"Hugh, could we shin up to the roof and block the chimney?"

At three stories high we could forget that idea but smoke and fire are synonymous with danger and if we could produce smoke, it would create a panic to get outdoors. Once outside, we could very quickly select our targets.

It seemed it was a plan that might work.

The long day was fast closing and darkness loomed as we neared the White Lion Inn. I took a risk and glanced inside to see how busy it was.

To my surprise and delight, there were few in the place and the reason was the presence of Bouchard and his men, displaying swords and weapons sufficient to terrorise the drinking patrons who had all quietly left.

Whispering to Hugh, "Swords..." somewhat cheekily, I nudged the bar door partly open and smiled at the nearest French assassin who ran to the door with his sword raised and ran straight into Hugh's cutlass. He was struck in the throat and fell twitching to the ground, very dead so we kicked him across the doorway. The next person out tripped over the carcass. I sliced his neck open and he met his end rather noisily. Then all hell broke loose.

Both doors crashed back and Bouchard, Snyder and the remaining five men attacked us with raised voices and vicious swings of their swords. Hugh and I stood back to back and fought together against these odds. My first assailant adopted a crouched fencing stance then attacked. I met him steel for steel and whilst he was good, he was quickly despatched thanks to my constant practice with Hugh who also dispatched his assailant very quickly.

Bouchard found me as I realised we were surrounded by troops with bayonets who stepped back to watch. Hugh's attacker hacked manfully as Bouchard went for me in raw furious anger. There was no sign of Snyder.

All my concentration was on the battle with Bouchard, who I noticed was letting his anger affect his swordplay, frequently rushing his moves in an attempt to rattle my defence.

Cold hard determination set into my sword play and I allowed Bouchard a little sense that I was more feeble than he believed. Slowly, remorselessly, I allowed him to attack and I fell back a little but he was tiring. Slowly and gradually I took the initiative and attacked again and again until he stumbled, fell and asked for mercy. I gave nothing and struck him a fatal blow.

Lowering my bloodied sword, I fell exhausted towards Hugh and we both watched, supporting each other, as our troops quickly gathered the bodies into a nearby cart, covered it with a canvas and disappeared into the gloom.

Mr Willoughby appeared silently at my shoulder, put his arm around me and whispered a very quiet, "Well done. We will see you both in my office please."

Once back at his premises, we endured his fulsome praise for our actions which would be handsomely rewarded, then we were summarily dismissed with orders to "Go home, you will be contacted". Mention was made of reimbursing my losses and a reward.

Outside in the darkness, Hugh and I looked at each

other, amazed that we had survived but now realising we were surplus to requirements and free to do as we pleased. Of course, even at that late hour, we found a tavern and drank ourselves stupid before we slept, fully clothed, in the bar and woke with two blinding headaches and a large bar bill to settle.

Outdoors in the morning air, we shook hands and parted, Hugh to meet Lady Arabella Forsythe, me to commence the long journey home to Brough.

CHAPTER 25
HEADING FOR HOME

Just by chance, you might say, I decided to visit Smithfield Market to connect with my coach for the journey home and of course as luck would have it, I just happened to be in the very tavern where I had been waylaid by the thieving ostlers.

I'd mentioned these rogues to Mr Willoughby who suggested I should use my code number to contact the local law officers and possibly identify these crooks and have them arrested. Before I visited the tavern, I agreed that two Constables would accompany me but at my suggestion they would wait outside and I would bring the rogues out to them. They seemed a little bemused with this but took a bench outside whist I wandered into the tavern.

Asking behind the bar for a small beer before I commenced my long trip home, I let slip that I had been most successful in my dealings with cattle that day but I needed a reliable coach to see me safely home.

It worked perfectly, my two cheerful ostlers appeared

and suggested we go into the nearby snug to discuss transport. Once inside and the door closed, I pointed to the small window and said, "Who's that?"

As they turned, I clashed their heads together, leaving them a little confused until I kicked them both between their legs and listened to them scream in pain, then I used my cudgel and broke both of their right wrists to rob them of their livelihood. As they blubbered and cried, I reminded them of their involvement in my robbery and the rope that would hang them.

The two Constables were quite taken aback at the state of their arrested miscreants and after having given a written account of my findings, they watched my departure to the coach with some relief.

So commenced the long stage coach trip back to the north and home, but first a stop in York.

CHAPTER 26
YORK AND SNYDER

Two very long days of travelling constantly by coach brought me to York and the Select Ladies Hat Shop of Miss Cornelia Elwick to discuss the purchase of good quality cattle to improve the stock in my farm in Westmorland. Locally the farmers were concentrating on dairy herds to fulfil the growing market in cities like York for fresh milk, which made me realise that by concentrating my efforts on a good herd of beasts for the meat market, I may be able to buy beasts locally that were not suitable for the dairy herd as my county had few large towns or cities nearby.

On arrival and after the usual pleasantries, I broached the subject with Cornelia who stated she could provide good contacts but suggested I may have another objective.

Her spies had noticed a recently arrived stranger who seemed to have money to burn and it was rumoured that the drovers had provided this windfall. Her spies confirmed it was that swine Snyder. But why was he so far north of his usual haunts?

My immediate concern was my family. Had Snyder tumbled to my background and wanted revenge?

Cornelia suggested we should track the man down, check his identity and deal firmly with him as she had it on good authority that he was a much sought after man. She bade me rest whilst she quickly left the shop, looking most determined.

Finding a quiet corner of the shop away from the other staff, I fell fast asleep in a comfortable chair to be woken four hours later with the offer of a cup of tea and a chat.

"I have a lot of information for you, Jack, some good and some very worrying." She proceeded to tell me that a good herd of cows that gave a heavy meat carcass were available for sale at a good price as they did not fit the farmers' need for a milking herd.

Fifteen beast were available at £8.00 each which was a very good price and I could drove them back to Brough the eighty odd miles in about eight to ten days provided I could get some labour. But Snyder was her great concern. He was last seen two days ago and appeared to be on a mission to extract revenge on a blasted northern farmer.

Making my decision very quickly, I asked Cornelia to agree the purchase of the cattle and I would return within ten days to pay and complete the transaction. Meanwhile, could she allow me to sleep overnight and help me to catch the early morning stagecoach heading to Edinburgh which would get me to Brough in two days with luck. I suspected that Snyder was hoping to cause distress at my house.

CHAPTER 27
GISELLE THREATENED AT HOME

Whilst coach travel is far easier than walking or riding on horseback, there is always the problem of mixing with other passengers who wish to talk on any subject. That's fine if you are socially aware but my dark mood thankfully prevented three elderly ladies from pressing me too hard. They were bound for Edinburgh on an excursion and very excited. Towns passed our window as we made steady progress on the Great North Road to Scotch Corner and then headed north west to Westmorland.

I was very anxious to reach home and was somewhat brusque with my friends who greeted me as I stepped off the stagecoach and ran to the nearest horse, grabbing its reins and swinging astride with my baggage. I set off, shouting, "Send me the bill, please."

Galloping up my long drive, my horse's hooves gave sufficient noise for Giselle to come flying out of the entrance door to greet me with tears of joy and a huge hug and kiss.

"Oh, Jack, my love, how we have all missed you so much."

Giles ran to join us and fell into my arms, squealing with delight. Then others tumbled from the house to hug, kiss and shake hands and I felt a wave of incredible happiness sweep over me at this affection.

We all trooped into the house, chattering noisily whilst I held Giselle's hand and kept Giles in my arms. I explained I had successfully bid on fifteen beef cows in York and would have to arrange for payment and collection shortly. Also I mentioned the prospect of Hector the bull being used as a stud animal to improve breeding in the York area and the considerable fees we could earn.

Cups of tea and hours later, I had all her news which was worse than I feared.

The Crozier family's demise had brought long lost cousins from Scotland to the area and they had started stealing my cattle in small numbers but regularly. Worse still, they had French connections who were outraged at the part I had played in the downfall of their rebellion and intended to make my life a misery, aided and helped by none other than Snyder. Using the tactics associated with the Reivers, it seemed the Croziers swooped at night, selected two or three beasts and drove them away to be slaughtered and sold immediately.

Including Snyder there were seven men involved who had a fearsome reputation according to local gossip. Already they were boasting of "Bettering Jack Rutherford" in the local taverns.

Their objective appeared to be a pitched battle on the streets of Brough where they would hope to outnumber me and extract vengeance.

Despite her concerns, Giselle insisted we had an early night which I thought a splendid idea.

CHAPTER 28
BRUTAL REVENGE

All my family were in fear of these men, having had insults and threats of violence thrown at them when shopping locally.

Cattle stealing is an offence punishable by hanging if convicted. Those who steal are well aware of this fact and act ruthlessly in their nefarious acts and will kill those who try to apprehend them. This makes the task of the local officers of the law very stressful and sometimes they turn a blind eye to rustling in case they become victims of these robbers.

I considered placing two good cows in a small enclosure with Hector the mad bull to encourage the robbers to attempt some stealing but the cows would be badly injured by the crazy bull and that would not work.

But to steal cattle you must first study the likely point from which to extract some beasts and then find a secure route to remove them out of sight. Supposing I could identify that route then any mishap befalling the thieves who were no longer on my land, could not be attributed to me, and the stolen cattle would be evidence itself of a misdemeanour.

Night time was when the thieving was taking place so very early in the morning after my return, I called my wolfhound Dag to accompany me and we slowly covered the whole of my farm. Dag is a great help at times but he can be a little headstrong. As you know, he is also a killer when asked.

Two possible routes from my furthest fields were identified as likely exits and on a thin path from my boundary, I noted cattle hoof prints in an area they would never normally appear. I would place a small herd of cows in the nearest pasture to this area and watch with great interest.

Over the next four days, Dag and I toured our land, looking at the cattle and sheep but keeping a watch on the area I identified as suspect and on the fourth morning, sure enough fresh boot marks likely from a reconnaissance gave me enough encouragement to return that night.

From my experience at least three men would be needed to accomplish this thieving task, all working independently, one leading, one at the side to prevent straying in to nearby paths and one at the rear, pushing the cattle along. Dag was worth his weight in gold on these ventures and I decided he and I would be capable of dealing with these people.

Once dark, I chose black clothing and took my heavy cudgel as well as the dirk in my boot.

We had many buildings on the estate and I had checked and prepared one stone byre that had housed pigs at one point and stank to high heaven. But it had no windows, a high roof and a very stout door that held a large padlock with the only key in my pocket.

Dag and I crept along the hedgerows that night and as we neared the escape path, I went on all fours after smearing my face and hands with mud to hide my pale skin. Old habits die hard.

Noises nearby confirmed my hope that this was the night they would strike. No voices but I could hear cattle stamping and jostling and then movement from the field as a piece of my fence was removed and four prime cows were brought out and led away.

As I anticipated, a front man leading the way, a middle man for control and a rear man pushing the beasts forward.

Once the rear man had closed the fence, he made to catch up but I hit him unconscious with a savage blow to the back of his neck. Dag was all for killing him but I whispered, "Lie down," and I then gagged and tied the villain.

Moving swiftly, I eventually caught up with the cows and was quietly admonished by the middle man who went very quiet once hit with my cudgel. Again, I gagged and tied him up.

The front man would be a challenge but I had a plan. I needed to find where they intended to take the beasts so that I could visit the next day and discuss things. So making appropriate noises as befits a middle herder, I allowed the dark to cover my movements.

Two hours later, we neared a small farm that I suspected belonged to Crozier interests but enough of that.

Moving past the cows, I came upon the leader and he succumbed quickly to a blow on the head after Dag caught his calf in his teeth and chewed. There was a considerable noise at first but it quietened down once he was unconscious and bound and gagged.

Strangely there was no activity at the farm so I left my four beasts in the farm yard and closed the gate.

I returned to my farm, saddled a mare to a small cart and retraced my steps, starting at the Crozier's farm where I loaded the first of my victims, then retraced my steps and collected the other two inert forms and threw them on the cart.

Finally, at home, I unlocked the pigsty door, threw the robbers in after untying their hands but leaving them gagged. Water in a bucket was in a corner and that was my concession to humanity.

It was 4am when I finally opened my door, and Dag and I were glad to just sit down and recover.

Next morning quite late, I strode with Dag to the pigsty to question my captives. Of course they had removed their gags and were all set to attack me but one growl from my dog and the sight of a blooded cudgel sent them back to the floor, whimpering.

They refused to give me any information and their

meal of dry bread and water seemed more than adequate, particularly when I suggested the man with the bite on his leg could soak up the blood with a crust.

My hope was that somebody would go to the Crozier farm to take the animals and I made haste after a quick breakfast to that place, with my dog, of course.

We approached from the town direction which was not a direct route from my house and my silent approach was correct. Two men had the four beasts on halters to take them for slaughter, I imagined.

Dag had the nearest man by the throat and his death scream so startled the second man that I was able to run him through with my dirk and left him in a pool of blood. No quarter was given, these were slaughtermen in every sense of the word.

Dag and I then herded my beasts back along the route we took the previous night and after two long hours my herd was intact again after an effective repair to the broken fence.

By my reckoning, this left a Crozier member and Snyder to deal with and I suspected they were in town in a tavern.

Arriving home, despite being bone weary, I saddled my horse, strapped on my sword and rode into Brough.

I greeted many people as I passed and some stared at my being armed with a sword. Dag had been told to say at home as he can be a little impatient.

I made for the Black Bull, dismounted, secured my horse and wandered into the tavern. Few patrons were in the bar and left rather quickly on my arrival. Moving into the restaurant, only two patrons remained, Snyder and someone I assumed was related to the Croziers, and they appeared a little concerned at my entry. Drawing my sword, I moved towards their table, watching for a pistol to appear.

Now somewhat pale, Snyder smiled complacently at me and suggested I was walking into serious danger, particularly when all his men would shortly appear.

He took the news of their capture or demise with a strong movement of his throat and showed some alarm. His companion however glanced at his wine glass and threw it at my face. But the action of his glance forewarned me and his action was anticipated and welcome. My drawn sword sliced into his chest and he was dead.

Snyder rose and drew his previously hidden sword with the comment, "Come on then, farm boy, and learn to die."

That remark gave me the idea that despite my aching body and tired mind, this man thought I was a beginner, so I acted that way as he attacked and slashed with enormous vigour.

He was a little taller than me and a capable swordsman so this would be a test of endurance and agility, but my constant practice with Hugh Sutcliffe gave me an advantage and my sword flashed as I parried the strokes of my opponent. I hated this man's guts because of his threats to my family.

As he attacked, he shouted, "My French connections will be the death of you. Your family will suffer long and hard once I have killed you. We French know of your property abroad."

I let him prattle on and tire himself with savage but useless thrusts. By the law of averages, he would eventually wound me and sure enough my left shoulder was cut, but not deep enough to draw blood which my assailant commented on with glee. Then I gave him a shoulder wound too.

All the time I retreated before his savagery, deliberately moving out of the restaurant, through the bar where I nearly lost my life tripping on a stool, then eventually into the street, just as I planned.

Of course, a crowd gathered very quickly with the noise when the hoarse voice of my assailant could be heard yelling, "Death to the upstart. France will prevail."

The local crowd muttered and formed a circle, but kept well clear.

Then slowly and remorselessly I started real fencing. I saw the startled look on his face as I transformed before his eyes from a common farmer to a born swordsman and a killer. Steadily and ruthlessly, I countered him at his every stroke, blocking his thrusts at my face, arms and legs with rapid defensive strokes learned in the hard school of survival.

Diagonal cuts, slashing cuts, inside hook thrusts, figure of eight motions came in rapid succession, all parried and negated by my defence until my opportunity came. I used my hack and thrust movement and went forward with the point of my sword, stopped briefly and then followed through to slash beneath his fighting arm and draw copious amounts of blood.

That was a telling cut and immediately weakened his fencing arm. He was tiring now and I should have been exhausted too but my cold fury meant I remained fully alert and ready to act.

I saw my opportunity as the severely weakened Snyder now stumbled on the cobbled street. I darted forward and gave him the killing stroke straight through his heart.

He died on the spot. Not a sound could be heard, not a murmur. A deathly hush. Blood, thankfully not mine, ran into the nearby gutter.

Finally, from the crowd, a minor town official stepped forward and to growing talk, thanked me for ridding the town of such foul criminals. As I wiped my sword clean and returned it to its scabbard, I suggested to the assembled people that I would now report to the Municipal authorities on what they had all seen and would give witness.

Home and my family were my immediate concern but first of all I stopped at the local Justices office with some of the more vocal bystanders and a Clerk wrote out my long statement, concerning my distress at the woeful lack of support for the law abiding people of Brough under Stainmore.

I deliberately gave the town its full official title and made it very clear in my statement given to the clerk that it was only on my return that any positive action had been taken.

Crozier family members had ruthlessly taken over, and law and order had disappeared. As a result, I wrote, it had fallen on me to track down the thieves who stole my cattle, three of whom were locked up on my land and were available for questioning after an arrest. Two slaughtermen could be found at the remote farm rented by the Crozier family but they had died, at my hand, when I attempted to recover my stolen cattle and they attacked me.

I then asked the Clerk to write out a copy of my statement. I waited a further hour as this was done, hovering over him like a hawk, until the replica was safely in my hands, duly witnessed by the two local men who had taken a keen interest in proceedings.

Exhausted and almost out on my feet, I mounted my horse and rode home.

CHAPTER 29
HOME TO MY FAMILY

My horse's steady plodding steps making for home allowed me to dwell on matters. Giselle would be furious with me for endangering myself again but as I approached the entrance to my small estate, there was a feeling of satisfaction at the end of a difficult task. No doubt I would hear shortly that all my costs would be met, as promised, giving me time to consider how best to bring those new cows back to my pastures.

It was now midday, I'd had little sleep and no food for over a day yet I was alive, the breeze was blowing in my hair and I felt justified in a brief smile.

Giles ran out of the house as I approached and I leapt from my horse and gathered him into my arms as he wriggled and questioned me, "Where have you been, Daddy?"

Giselle appeared at that moment and looked quizzically at me as I attempted a suitable reply.

"To be truthful, Giles, I have been collecting some cows that may have strayed," I admitted.

"Yes, Giles, Daddy has been very busy and he is going to tell Mummy and you all about it right now and explain this important letter from the government that has been placed in my personal care."

That Home Office sealed letter proved to be of such interest to Giselle that her questioning my behaviour eased after ten minutes and she suggested I open the missive, in her presence but in our office.

The Office of the Secretary of State for the Home Office had penned a letter couched in gloriously vague terms. It suggested that as Mr Jack Rutherford had provided valuable information to the government some recognition should be made.

Therefore, a sum of £3,000 had been allocated to defray expenses. Further, following a recent death of a landholder in the area, local Solicitors had advised that land would be forfeit to the government as no heirs had been identified.

It is customary for the government to take over these lands and run them for a profit to the nation's benefit. However, in this case, the land appeared to have no value but it was noted it practically abuts onto land owned by Mr J. Rutherford. Due to the high cost of maintaining this sixty acres of scrubland, in view of services rendered to the government, it would be offered to Mr J. Rutherford for a nominal amount of one pound sterling. It would please the writer to have a prompt response. It was signed Mr. K. J. Willloughby, Chief Clerk.

This quite took my breath away as it did to Giselle who

looked very surprised at me with a comment of, "What's been going on here, Jack?"

"I was robbed in Smithfield Market," I explained. "I had collected my money, paid off all our men and told Dag and the other dogs to 'Go home'. Then as I was preparing to get the coach, I was given a 'spiked' drink."

At that, Giselle looked concerned but waited patiently for me to continue.

"I was robbed of our money and left in a field," I said. "Fortunately, that wild dog of mine had disobeyed my orders, followed the robbers and so was able to help in my escape. Turns out I had inadvertently become involved in a wider issue."

Giselle raised her beautiful French eyebrows at my mention of the word 'inadvertently' but she let me finish.

"Seems I was able to give some assistance to the government and they want to thank me." I waved towards the letter in her hand. "So that's all well and good. However," I said, and went on to remind her that we would shortly take delivery of a small herd of beef cows and that Hector, the bull, was wanted for stud duties in York, for a big set of fees.

At this point, Giselle mentioned a sheep herd she had successfully acquired which made a lot of sense for our future farming prospects but then commented that of course we would need to travel to York and that successfully led to a conversation about dress making and huge profits, completely forgetting the matters in London.

Later that evening as we snuggled in front of the fire, I was able to ask Giselle how she was feeling this evening.

"Very pregnant," was such a wonderful surprise that I was able to forget for some time the threat that Snyder had shouted before he died...

BIBLIOGRAPHY

Bonser. K. J. *The Drovers, who they were and how they went.*

Haldane. A.R.B. *Drove Roads of Scotland.*

Calloway, Chuck. *Sword Skills.*

Walker, George. *The Costume of Yorkshire*

Walling, Phillip. *Counting Sheep. A Celebration of the Pastoral Heritage of England.*

Coldstream Guards: *Waterloo. Weapons and Warfare.*

Wikipedia.

British Battles.com *Battle of Waterloo.*

With kind assistance.

Vanessa Wells Chilli Fox Design, Hampshire.

Brian and Julie Cook.

The Robinson House Writers.